THE DJINN'S APPLE

THE DJINN'S APPLE

Djamila Morani

translated by Sawad Hussain

NEEM TREE
PRESS

Published by Neem Tree Press Limited, 2024

Originally published in Arabic as تفاحة الجن in 2017 by دار منشورات المثقف

Copyright © Djamila Morani, 2017

Translation Copyright © Sawad Hussain, 2024

1 3 5 7 9 10 8 6 4 2

Neem Tree Press Limited

95a Ridgmount Gardens, London, WC1E 7AZ

United Kingdom

info@neemtreepress.com

www.neemtreepress.com

A catalogue record for this book is available from the British Library.

ISBN 978-1-911107-85-9 Paperback
ISBN 978-1-911107-86-6 Ebook
ISBN 978-1-911107-28-6 Ebook US

This book has been selected to receive financial assistance from English PEN's "PEN Translates" programme

Printed and bound in Great Britain.

To those whom I taught so they could pass exams…
You all taught me how to make it in life.

For my students, 2009-2016.

Grandma Djamila

If the Djinn's Apple was asked, which would you rather be: a blessing or a curse—who knows what it would choose!

Table of Contents

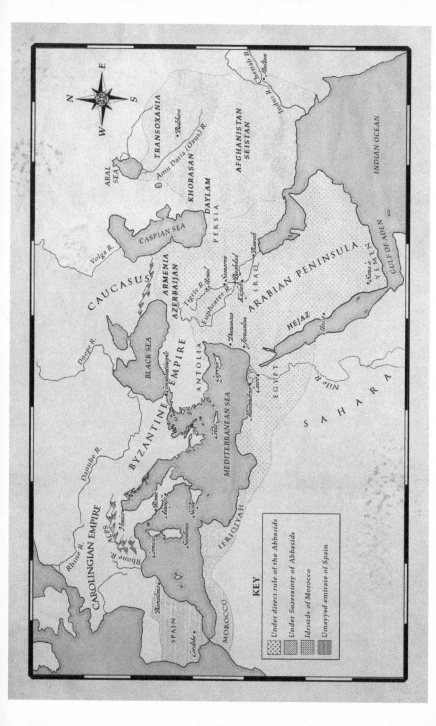

The Djinn's Apple

PART 1

Chapter 1

My siblings' screams still pierce my ears no matter how hard I squeeze my head between my hands. Their cries ring out, filling my head until it almost bursts.

I'm recalling that day so long ago. It had started like any other with the meuzzin's early morning call to prayers sounding across Baghdad—the most opulent city in the world they said—and my home.

I'm curled up in my bed as I hear Laween and Rohan arguing in the hallway. Rohan must have been dragging his feet to get to prayer like he always did, and the last thing Laween would want is to upset my father. My mother's head pops out from behind the door, and she's surprised to see me awake.

"Here you are! Your father is waiting for you so we can pray. Hurry up!"

"Okay, okay," I say as I lift my blanket off my body. But instead of getting ready right away, I pause by my window and open it. I fill my lungs with the scent of basil grown just below—my favourite way to start the morning. How could I do anything different when we have a garden with plants of all shapes and colours? Maybe this house isn't as big as our last one in downtown Baghdad, but having this garden makes it the most beautiful place to be—a haven after we escaped with our lives from the caliph's constant threats.

And then that night disaster struck.

I couldn't see anything in the dark; the moon hidden behind the clouds, embarrassed by what it might see or hear. I felt my way through the willow trees, my father's face coming into focus as he opened the back gate to our house. "Go, now," he ordered. "We'll be right behind you. I've got to get your siblings and mother." He shoved me out and shut the garden gate, but I didn't budge. How could I leave knowing that he was going back to die?

We had been in his study, Baba as usual transcribing something or other while I gazed curiously at a strange manuscript, the candle in the hanging lantern casting flickering shadows on the parchment. "Leave that manuscript alone and finish your reading, Nardeen," he scolded. Tugging on my bottom lip, I stared at the odd drawing on the page, which kind of looked like a human: it had four limbs that seemed like arms and legs and a small circle that could have been a head.

"What's this, Baba? Did a child draw it?"

He cut me off with a sternness I wasn't used to. I raised my book in front of my face, pretending to read the words, while my eyes stayed glued to that manuscript...but the next thing I knew, a powerful boom shook the room, causing the book to slip from my hands.

"Al-Rashid's men! Al-Rashid's men!"

The name of Harun Al-Rashid echoed in every part of our large house, a name that spelled our death. Strange, seeing how—just a few weeks before—it had meant the life we had always dreamed of.

It's hard to wrap your mind around the fine line between life and death.

Sometimes it's so thin you can barely tell the difference.

I rushed to the balcony and craned forward to see men with their swords drawn, chanting, "Kill the apostates! Kill the infidels!" They didn't look anything like Al-Rashid's guards. *How did they find us?* Flinching at their voices, I turned to my father, who had jumped up from his chair when he heard the word "apostates". He grabbed my hand and dragged me behind him down the stairs, his eyes surveying the area before him. He turned round to look at me. My eyes clung to the fear I had seen in his. I pulled on his hand and mumbled, "Baba..."

He stumbled but didn't stop. I pressed my small palm into his sweaty one. Fear, for me, at twelve years old, was usually a bogeyman from my mother's stories chasing me; he would melt away, disappearing completely, whenever I ran into my father's arms. But this fear that had blanketed Baba's eyes was uglier than any bogeyman. He opened the back door and pushed me out harshly towards the garden gate. I tried to open the door again, but Baba had locked it from the inside.

I stood on the doorstep, listening to the sounds of bodies and things crashing to the floor; my brother and sister yelling; everyone calling out for everyone else, but nobody answering, like they couldn't hear each other. Bayan's loud wail...I could pick her out in the middle of the storm of shouting. Usually her cries were loud and annoying, but now it was a desperate wail that tore my heart up. A loud wail that didn't belong to her five-year-old self. Suddenly she fell silent. The quiet slithered slowly all through the house and garden, and the voices fell away. I only heard the cautious, firm steps that Death itself took inside, searching, it seemed, for another life, the final one to snatch before it left the place. My grip on the door handle loosened and I pushed my ear up against the door.

"Sire...I've looked for her everywhere."

"She *must* be here, look harder," Death ordered.

My knees felt weak. I backed down a few steps. My foot slipped and I fell. *Are they looking for me?*

"I told you, keep looking!" Death yelled.

I stared at the shut door and imagined it opening. I sprinted outside the garden, not looking right or left—if I glanced back even once, Death would swallow me whole. I ran without knowing where I was going, my feet leading me to a nearby mosque. I used to love looking up at the lamps that hung from chains along the streets, watching as they swayed in the wind and the dancing light guided us along the path. But that night, I did not look up even once.

8

I steadied myself against the wall and sank to the ground to catch my breath, my heart pounding so wildly it felt like it was going to burst out of my chest. I caught sight of the ink that had drawn a line along the length of my hand. A reminder of another life when I sat with my father making notes in my book while he talked. It looked like henna, actually, just like the henna of the Bedouin women! I remembered the face of that woman Anan, the dark Bedouin soothsayer, whose hand was dyed with henna—she had visited Mama a few days before. A cold shiver travelled through my body, without me knowing why. Was it the cold night wind or what she had said?

"This land is no longer for the likes of you all; everything that was for you will be against you, Bani Yahya. All of you will drown in blood." Anan was sitting on the divan along one side of the room and I was sitting near Bayan's bed with my book.

My mother, Qasma, raised her hand to stifle the gasp that nearly slipped out. Catching herself, she went to the bed to check that little Bayan was still sleeping soundly. She didn't want my baby sister to hear what awaited her, what awaited the Baramika people in the coming days. I pretended to be absorbed in my reading but spied her normally clear grey eyes grow dark, her brow furrowed. She returned to her spot facing Anan. "Oh God…have mercy," she whispered under her breath. Out loud she added, "But the Baramika in the

9

caliph's entourage have already been severely punished, and my husband's friends promised that they would protect us."

"If only devotion could stop death, then the most devoted of us would never die, my lady. But the final hour is victorious, and the appointed time isn't in my hands. I'm just sharing the message to the best of my knowledge."

My mother gasped, her face pale.

My mother had thought, as my father had, that disappearing from the angry caliph's sight—and that of his entourage—would protect our family from any danger. She didn't understand why the soothsayer was all doom and gloom. Even if we were of the Baramika family line, we were as far as we could possibly be from its politics and all that went along with it. Baba had chosen the medical profession, studying at Bimaristan medical school in Baghdad. He wasn't like the rest of the Baramika men who had served the Abbasids, one caliph after the other. All that tied him to the family line was his last name, and the wealth he had inherited from my grandfather.

When Harun Al-Rashid's relations with the Baramika turned sour, things got so tough for Baba in Bimaristan that he had to leave his post and stay at home. Everyone in the royal court was pointing the finger at each other. With so many accusations swirling, people's lives were being turned upside down. Everyone seemed to be constantly looking over their shoulders, Harun Al-Rashid especially. And when the nobles in important positions, including even one of the caliph's closest cousins, started getting murdered—no one had a clue who the murderer was!

During those troubled days, all Baba cared about was protecting us from the caliph's outpouring of fury that had crushed Baramika lives without a second thought. Maybe the caliph himself hadn't ordered their slaughter, but he left them up for grabs for whoever wanted to attack them. Baba tried to calm Mama's fears, but her heart told her that the soothsayer's words were our inevitable fate. A fate that opened its arms, called out to us, waiting for us. A fate that became our shadow, staying with us until it scooped us up once and for all into its arms.

I used to eavesdrop whenever Mama invited one of her soothsayers over. I liked listening to the web of lies that they were so good at spinning, so that I could share them with my father when he came home in the evening. Not for one second did Baba believe what they came up with. "Even when soothsayers are telling the truth, they're lying," he'd say, his eyes never leaving the book in his hands. But he couldn't get Mama to drop the habit that was so popular with the Abbasid women, and their men too, with soothsayers reaching the courts of kings and caliphs. The strange thing was that Anan wasn't like the rest: she didn't dress up her prophecies or fill her lies with dried-up hope. Instead, she snapped her vision out like a whip, the crack in the air more painful than where it actually landed. Like this, her words were terrifying long before they might have come true.

Anan scattered her stones on a patch of black fabric—which was meant to show the way forward—shaking her head, listening for the evil spirits that had just fled the heavenly kingdom, arriving with stolen bits of news. She swatted the air as if to get rid of something and opened her eyes as wide as they would go, trying to see what was hidden behind the screen of the unknown. Hugging herself, she murmured, "A sea of darkness will drown everyone, a black fury is coming."

"How can we all be punished for one man's sin?"

"O child of Yahya Al-Baramika, family is a necklace; if it comes loose, all its beads will fall."

With a trembling hand Qasma wiped the sweat dripping down her forehead. The Abbasid caliph was raging against the Baramika, the same people who had grown up alongside him, provided stability, supported him, shouldered the burdens of the nation, advised him, defended him; those same people were now his worst enemies, and his first victims. Why? A question that was out of place, it seemed. Politics has a beautiful side that charms men who fall into her clutches and worship her, giving her everything they have. But she's also a woman with secrets too holy to divulge, desires too ugly to speak aloud, promises like sandcastles crumbling under the waves of her fury. If she showed them her true face with all its adornment, their souls would be the sacrifice.

"Even when soothsayers are telling the truth, they're lying," I repeated to myself while a lantern's shadow danced on the mosque wall. *The soothsayers told the truth, Baba, they told the truth even though they're lying.*

I hugged my legs to my chest, rested my head on my knees, and cried. That stupid prophecy had come true: my family was scattered, our peace of mind gone. Our lives were a living hell. In the few weeks that had passed, my life and that of every Baramika descendant had been turned upside down. Just a few days had been enough to either humiliate everyone or drag them to an awful death. My parents had been worried about us, telling my siblings and me not to go outside the house. Even friends no longer dropped by, afraid prying eyes would get them in trouble with the caliph. One by one, they all slipped away, leaving my father and our family to face death alone.

Chapter 2

Allahu Akbar… Allahu Akbar…

The dawn call to prayer rang out, announcing the start of a new day. *Why, then, did I still feel like it was yesterday, my feet still stuck there? Why could I still hear them screaming?* I looked at the men starting to gather at the mosque. One of them leaned over me. "Are you alright?"

I looked up at him, considering his face, darkened by the lantern's dancing shadow. As I tried to make sense of what had just come out of his mouth, my eyelids grew heavy. I didn't answer him, his words not meaning anything. Was he speaking a different language? "Have you come to pray?" the man pressed.

I jumped from my place as if bitten by a rattlesnake. His words seemed strange. *Pray? What about those I had left behind? Had they prayed? Baba didn't like it if we were late to pray.* I rushed home, barely aware of the city waking up around me. Mama's face came to mind, biting her lip as she always did when scolding me: "Look at your clothes, Nardeen! It's not right for a Baramika girl as beautiful as you to go around in dirty clothes like these!"

I dusted the dirt off my robes and smiled. *Mama must be waiting for me at home, ready to tell me off for how I look.* "You're a woman now," she always insisted. "You won't get anything out of those books, *binti*. If only you put some kohl around your eyes, you'd drive the men crazy. Men were made to use their brains and women to look pretty," she would say as she combed her long brown hair to rest on her shoulders. "Your lovely eyes will waste away for no reason. You know Baramika girls don't belong in medical school!"

"Men are the doctors," she always rattled on. "They may put their hearts in the hands of a beautiful woman, but they don't trust her brain to treat the smallest of their wounds." She had twisted round to me, my frowning face meeting hers. She had gestured for me to come closer, and had wrapped her arms round my waist, giving me a peck.

"Don't be upset now." On my forefinger she had slipped on a silver ring. Bending down to my feet, she had tied a silver anklet with shiny coins dangling from it. "Just a jangle from our anklets, and people know that we women are around. It announces our presence, and draws everyone's attention to us in this world ruled by men."

⌐◞

I slowed down on my way home, going over her words. I looked at my ring and then shook my left ankle, the jangling

16

sound put me at ease. I'm here alright. The jewellery round my anklet confirmed that I'm still in this world, still breathing. The sound of it cheered me up, being alive cheered me up. It meant that everyone else is fine, they've got to still be alive. I sped up towards the house again, but then stood still at a distance. *I told you, keep looking!* I rubbed the back of my neck. Were those men still looking for me?

Peeking out from behind the houses, the sun lit up the path I walked on. It seemed like a safe, quiet road, nothing like the road of horror that I had sprinted down just yesterday. Seeing a crowd of people in front of the house, I exhaled in relief. They must be there to help us. I slipped in between them, trying to get to the door. One of them cupped his hands together, shaking his head. "God save us. Even the children weren't spared!"

Someone else jabbed him. "The fate for all infidels is death. Whoever murdered our lord Musa bin Ja'far deserves to die."

"But what did the children have to do with this?" the other man moaned.

"Evil begets evil."

Who was he calling evil? My father?

My stomach was in knots. I remembered my sister Bayan wailing, and then falling silent. My knots grew tighter. I tried to ignore them, elbowing my way through the crowd that stood witnessing the end of our supposed infidel Zoroastrian family. I walked towards the door, trying to understand how that man could call my father an infidel? How, when he'd scold me time and again when I put off

17

prayer. Or how when I hadn't finished memorizing a surah, he'd stop me from going into his library. Hadn't they seen all the charity Baba gave to keep the needy going hungry? Didn't they see how he treated poor sick people for free? My father, a man of skill, passionate about remedies and how to make them, had never harmed a single soul in his life. How could they go on like this about him, his family, his religion? An infidel?!

Known for his love of books, my father insisted we read everything we could get our hands on. He spent hours in the *Bayt-Al-Hikma*. Learning about other ways of life and cultures was important to him. He was so proud of our Persian roots that he gave us all classic Persian names: Rohan, Laween, Nardeen, Bayan.

He'd always say, "In Baghdad, you've got to be Arab to be Abbasid. You all are just as Muslim as them. Your names represent your identity, not your religion."

Not satisfied with us just reading at home, he called tutors over who'd stand in for him when he got too busy translating medical books. But I caught my father's attention. My memory was incredible—I never forgot a single word I read. I had memorised more than ten medical books already, and I wasn't even ten years old. My father was astonished, but it made my mother wring her hands. "I don't want her stuck in these books. Just look at her. She's not eating, she's barely drinking. All she does is go to the library and read."

"You should be happy, she's memorised more than her siblings. If you weren't so against it, I'd be getting her ready for Bimaristan admission."

"The granddaughter of Mohammed Bin Yahya Al-Baramika at Bimaristan? Every day you wash blood off your hands, you touch the sick and the infected. Aren't two sons enough for this career of yours?"

"Al-Baramika, Al-Baramika, I swear to God you're obsessed with this family name."

Baba stopped sending the tutor to me, not because he was afraid of my grandfather, but out of worry for me. He knew how big my dreams were, and that this world wasn't ready for a girl with dreams like mine. But he stayed devoted as ever to me, never losing interest for even one day. I remember well how every evening he'd pick me up in his strong arms and place me in the seat facing him. Teaching me the names of herbs, the benefits of certain remedies, the symptoms of specific illnesses, their causes and treatments. I sensed that he talked constantly to lessen the guilt he felt for stopping my studies. But, actually, Baba's evening sessions were better than my teachers' lessons had ever been, never leaving any of my questions unanswered.

"Baba, have any of your patients died because you gave them the wrong medicine?"

My father stopped crushing the seeds. He picked them up to make sure they were fine enough, then dusted the remainder off his fingers. "Doctors evaluate, but death at the end of the day is all in God's hands."

"I don't get it."

"What I mean is, doctors try their best to keep patients alive. There's nothing wrong Nardeen with a patient dying after you've done all you can. Now if you don't try hard enough, that's a different matter."

Chapter 3

"No one should help bury these atheists." The blood rushed to my head and my cheeks grew hot. I started to make my away again through the crowd to my house. "Get out of my way!" I screeched.

I stumbled upon a faint aroma that welcomed me when I made my way through the door. A sweet smell that didn't make sense with all this rotten death in the house. Where was this sweet smell coming from? I could barely find a place to stand. Everything was upside down. I leaned against the smooth wall to take it all in. Silk pillows lying on the floor. The mother-of-pearl and ivory sofa now in two. My mother would be furious if she had seen our house like this. Was that our Persian carpet? Mud and straw now hid the once beautiful patterns.

I walked deeper inside, something sticky under my feet. I looked at the tiles and saw the stains—the blood stains.

Whose blood was it? Was it my sister's? I panicked and fell to the ground. My hands and clothes now stained red. I scrubbed my hands trying to remove the bloodstains, but it just spread even more. Tears fell when I thought of whose blood it could be, their faces spinning round me, squeezing the air out of me.

I heard the sound of glass breaking in my father's room and pulled myself together to get there. My legs were heavier with every step on the staircase as I neared the top. I forced my feet to shuffle to the doorway, my heart hammering in my chest. I saw three men turning the room upside down from top to bottom, stealing anything worth taking. What they should have been focused on was under their feet: my father's medical books and his priceless manuscripts, crushed by their sandals. What a nightmare, these fascinating words and ideas now dirty under the feet of people who didn't know any better. Groaning, dying, disappearing. I shoved one of the men with both hands, and tried to save the last souls in this house that were drowning in death. The only weapon I had left was my voice. At the top of my lungs I ordered, "GET OUT! GET OUT!"

One of them bent down to me while I herded the books on the floor together. He stared at me. "Aren't you Hazeer's girl?"

His voice was familiar. I looked up at him and recognised him immediately. He was one of Al-Aasefi's servants. His master would always send him to our place to collect the books that my father had translated from Syriac to Arabic. His master was the one who had accused my father of plotting to kill the caliph's cousin. I looked at him hard, trying to figure out why he was here, in our house, at a time like this. He grabbed me roughly by the shoulders, and pulled me up, so I was standing before him. He waved a manuscript in my face. For just a moment, I couldn't make out which one it was because I'd seen so many in Baba's library. But then, my eyes widened when I saw the drawing that looked like a human body: four limbs spread out, and a head at the top of the manuscript. I balled up my long thawb in my fist tightly, remembering my parent's fight last week, the day after Anan the soothsayer visited the house.

My father had been pacing back and forth in the wood panelled room, with book-filled shelves lining each wall, removing books from where they were, and then putting them back again. He inspected his wooden chest decorated with ivory. Something valuable must be missing—that's what all of us thought. But no one dared to ask. His face was twisted, and his nostrils flared. Rohan and Laween were in the middle of the room observing his movements. Bayan and I were at the door, peeking our heads in to get a better look. We each wanted to help, but we didn't know how. Baba didn't say a word. Rohan took the plunge. "What are you looking for?"

"If you tell us, we can all have a look for it!" Laween added.

Baba stopped searching and glanced over at his two anxious sons. He realised just how stumped we were by his behaviour. Taking a moment to collect himself, he sat down on his chair, and pointed to the chest. "Did any of you touch this?"

Rohan and Laween looked at each other in confusion. They shook their heads. My father then pulled out a manuscript. "There were two manuscripts in this chest: one in Arabic, and the other in Syriac. This here is the Syriac one, so where's the Arabic one?"

Both boys got closer to the manuscript. "Never seen it before," Rohan declared. Laween nodded furiously in agreement. But I had seen it, and I couldn't keep quiet.

"It's…" Everyone turned to look at me. Baba came close.

"Have you seen it before, Nardeen?"

"I…"

"Tell me Nardeen. Speak up, my girl. Have you seen it before?"

I fell silent.

"I'm the one who took the second manuscript," my mother interjected, striding across the room towards us. "Yes, I got rid of it," she confessed, pushing me out of the way.

"Don't you ever get tired?" my father snapped. "That translation could have kept us safe."

"I'm protecting my children from all this." She waved her hands around. "I just want their safety, while all day long you've got your nose in these books and damned manuscripts. Al-Aasefi wants that manuscript, that's why he accused you of trying to kill Al-Rashid's cousin, so just give it to him. Just give him everything. That man won't leave us alone. It's not just today that Al-Rashid turned his back on us Baramika, you know."

"You have no idea what you've done Qasma! You've condemned us all!" She had barely finished what she was saying when he roared at her, and she dropped to the floor. Bayan screamed while I hurried to Mama.

Stunned, Rohan pulled at my father to keep him back, and begged him. "Please. No more. Please."

⌇

I woke up to a hard slap from Al-Aasefi's servant. He yanked me out of my thoughts. "The Arabic manuscript. Tell me where it is."

Stay strong, Nardeen. Strong and silent.

It was that same manuscript, the one written in a language that wasn't Arabic, the one that Baba was guarding these past few days, saying it proved he was innocent. Yes, it's that one. But I wouldn't dare open my mouth, the last time I did, my father flew off the handle. Wouldn't it be the same if I told Al-Aasefi's servant anything now?

The servant rolled up his sleeves, his eyes cold. He punched me in my stomach, and I found myself falling to my knees on the floor clutching my arms around my body for protection. He kicked me over and over, and then stamped on me…I held my breath while he screeched breathless, "Where is it? Where is it?" My mouth had sealed shut, like stone. I tried as hard as I could to keep the one last secret I had deep down. Gradually my breath started to slow down. Everything around me turned black. His blows and insults didn't hurt me anymore, I no longer felt anything.

The only thing I saw was my father's hand outstretched towards me, his face lighting up the darkness. But instead of reaching out for him, I turned my face away and shifted towards the sweet smell; the smell of death that welcomed me at the door.

I needed to know where this smell came from. Some people yearn to live, others yearn to die. We shake Death's hand wanting to examine his face critically, to make a note of his features. In my delirium, I found myself yearning for Death, his sweet smell tempting me to get nearer, nearer still, to see him up close and personal. He didn't seem all that scary, he was quite familiar actually, he looked like...was it Al-Aasefi's face? No...it was the devil himself.

Did you sleep well that night, Al-Aasefi? After you washed your hands of my father's blood. I'd never hear my father laugh again. *Did you touch your children with your guilty hands? Did you kiss them?* Without Baba's goodnight kiss, I can't sleep. The questions bounce off one another, screaming in my head, demanding to be fed. But the answers I have are so thin, so meaningless, they'll never be enough.

⁓

"They were killed because they're Zoroastrians, infidels."

"No, it's because they're Baramika and they had a hand in the murder of Al-Rashid's cousin."

"This family? But the Commander of the Faithful never ordered for them to be murdered. The Muslim extremists must be responsible."

Why couldn't someone just give me a straight answer? Why were they murdered? How can it be so easy for someone to kill another human, then so hard for them to come up with one reason to explain why?

Chapter 4

Two days passed. Everyone around me thought I was unconscious, but I simply didn't want to open my eyes. I didn't want to open them, scared of what I might see: a life without my parents. With my eyes closed I could still see them, alive, smiling at me, waving from a distance. My father there in his room, reading some book or another, always reading, to the point that I thought reading was another religious duty that he carried out without fail, just like his five prayers. What would I do if I opened my eyes and they weren't there? What would I do if I opened my eyes and made out that crack in the wall of my life, reminding me with every sunrise, its rays stealing through, that an earthquake had struck my family that night.

For my father, Hazeer, life could be summarised in two words: yes or no. He wasn't a man who stood in the middle. No sort of current pulled him along, and he never shied away from the word "no" if it was a crime to say "yes". That's what he had done ever since he was a young man, when he had said "no" to my grandfather. "I don't want to stay here; I don't want to be a part of this."

My grandfather had married him off to one of Mohammed Bin Yahya Al-Baramika's daughters, so that he could get closer to their family. My grandfather had the money, but he didn't have the right social connections. For his not so well-known family, he was searching for a position next to one of Mohammed Bin Yahya's sons in the royal court. Hazeer disobeyed when my grandfather ordered him to join Al-Rashid's court. He was the only one with a conscience when he stood up to the rolling thick fog that everyone else was stuck in. For God's sake, how could all those people at the court live in such a fog? How could they breathe, or make things out at all? How could they even speak without their words boomeranging back to suffocate them?

Baba was unable to lie to or sweet talk anyone—and though he was quick-tempered, he was honest, loyal, and reliable. The caliph didn't need consistency in his entourage though, politics didn't need it. Instead, being able to go with the flow was needed, being as flexible as possible, so as not to break. My father couldn't risk doing what the Baramika men did, diving deep into the belly of the kingdom, mastering the game of politics, only to end up becoming its victims. My grandfather put a whole lot of pressure on my father to quit

30

medicine and his books, and to make himself available to the court, but the only thing my father feared was that mysterious place. Being so consistent and reliable though made him lose his life, and all of ours too.

⁓

"Open your eyes" my father yelled at me. My weary body jolted, and I opened my eyes looking for him, but he had disappeared. Was I hallucinating? I tried to sit up and felt something crawling under my skin on all my limbs. My entire body was numb. My head feeling heavy, I slowly looked around where I was: a tidy room wrapped in antiseptic smell. It seemed familiar...I was in Bimaristan! A horrific pain gnawed at my left arm. I pulled back the white sheet and saw the cast covering it. I stared at it, trying to remember what had happened. It had all been a bad dream...yes, just a bad dream. But my broken arm, the bruises all over my body, said otherwise.

I was barely conscious of what was around me, drowning in a whirlpool of fever. My body would shiver now and again, sheets of sweat pouring off from me. I knew these symptoms very well. I felt a gentle cool hand touch my forehead. "Oh God, her fever is back. What should I do?"

"Try again nurse," said the flabby man next to her.

The nurse sat me up and tried to get me to drink something. But it was no use. My mouth was sealed, refusing everything. She pleaded with me, her voice soft, that I should listen to her and help her save my life. Little did she know I'd already given up on this world. Her pleading tired me out a great deal. My head was already ringing with Bayan's unending screams. It started to throb even more. I tried to block my ears with my right arm, maybe the pain would ease a bit, but the nurse kept on pleading. A sharp exclamation burst out of my chest. I couldn't keep it bottled in. I flung the clay bowl and it crashed against the wall, the liquid inside pouring on the ground. Those in the room grew flustered. No one moved. I had shut them up.

"What's going on here?"

From behind the nurse, a short old man appeared. His back was hunched and his beard was so red it could have been on fire; making his face more flushed. His already small-set eyes became slits when he looked at me. "Omayma, keep in mind there's a patient next door."

"I'm sorry but the girl is beyond stubborn, she doesn't listen to anyone. She's not eating or drinking."

I saw his lips press into a resolute straight line. When he stroked his beard, the reflection of his golden ring blinded me an instance. He went past the nurse and approached the small table on my right. He picked up a glass of laban and handed it to me.

"You've got to eat something."

I pushed the salted yogurt drink away and yelled, "I want to see Al-Aasefi. I've got to see him!"

The old man's eyes widened. He turned to the nurse asking for an explanation.

"Muallim Ishaq, she's the doctor's daughter, you know what happened…"

Each of us looked at the other, he was just as surprised as I was! Muallim Ishaq was a professor and a respected scholar of medicinal herbs. What this man had written and shared in his lessons was equal to what all the Bimaristan doctors had written combined. There was no plant or remedy that he hadn't written about in generous detail. Rohan and Laween would never miss a lesson of his, and his name would be on everyone's lips for days in the house. It was the dream of every student in Bimaristan to study with him, so how was I behaving like this in front of him? Seeing him turn around about to leave, I swallowed hard. I grabbed at his cloak that reached down to his ankles and mumbled, "I want to see Al-Aasefi."

Professor Ishaq turned back to me and clasped my hand. "You should be focusing on getting better, not Al-Aasefi. If you stay like this, you'll be dead before you get the chance." Shifting to Nurse Omayma he went on before leaving, "Don't give her the medicine until she's finished all her soup."

"Will she be okay? I mean, will she be able to use her arm again?"

I took notice of the square-shouldered man who had just asked this question, standing next to the nurse, concerned about my wellbeing. At such moments where we feel so alone, like a piece of straw floating lost, we search for familiarity in any of the faces around us. I squeeze my memory to find some scene with this man, some link, but nothing. His puffy face, thick lips, and dull features didn't help me remember anything. I lay my head on the pillow and closed my eyes once more.

The man begged, "Sayyid Ishaq, I've got to take her with me today. The market is booming at this time of year."

"Do it then, take her now if you want. But I won't give you my approval as a doctor. I've never seen anyone have their cast removed only after two days and then be able to move their arm around. You won't gain anything by selling her as a slave when she can't even pour a drink for her master," he said while using a rag to wipe away what was left of the laban on his hands, seemingly indifferent.

"But that'll set me back, and the other slave traders will smell my blood in the water. My customers will be upset too. Luckily, she's a looker…maybe they'll wait for her."

"Two weeks, and you'll get your slave girl. Working arm, grey eyes, and all. Her looks won't do you any good if her arm stays like this."

The slave trader and Muallim Ishaq disappeared from my view, their words still in the air. A slave! The word sunk into me, grew thick and then black. This blackness filled the room, and I couldn't see anyone. A Baramika descendant, a slave? If you could only hear this Mama, your daughter to be sold in the slave market tomorrow. Who'll tell them that the Baramika were made to be masters?

Who will care about another Baramika being sold or killed? I'm just like any other Baramika now: cursed, thrown out from Al-Rashid's heaven. What crime did I commit? What forbidden fruit did I take a bite of? Questions that will stay with me till my final breath. The heaven that I had been dying to get into—Bimaristan, medical school—was the end goal for me, and my brothers: Rohan and Laween. Today its doors were shut to me. All the books I had read, all the plants whose names I had memorised staying up late with my father, all the dreams I had piled up one atop the other, all gone up in smoke.

I wiped away the sweat that dotted my face and picked up the glass next to me. *Don't taste before you smell,* my father would say, as a warning against tasting any remedy before looking at its colour and smelling it. Tasting isn't a choice but a risk that could take a doctor's life. Inside this dark glass, I couldn't make out the colour of the drink, so I'd have to depend on smelling it. A heady smell wafted up from the glass, the smell of boxthorn, maybe? I brought it closer to my nose, and then Omayma rushed towards me, in a panic. "No! No! Don't drink that." She grabbed it from my hand.

"This smells like boxthorn but stronger."

"How do you know that?" She put the glass on the table and was taken aback. "Is your rude master always with you?"

"My master?"

"The man who was here a little while ago, he said you're his slave."

"I don't remember being anyone's slave."

"But aren't you Baramika?"

"And have the Baramika become slaves?"

The nurse sat down and started applying the ashes to my various wounds, her head lowered. She didn't answer. I didn't really need one anyway. The whole of Baghdad had come to know that there was no promise of security for the Baramika from the caliph. My tears started to mix with the ashes, leaving black drops on the floor, which was enough of an answer.

35

Chapter 5

Two weeks passed by quickly. During that time, I didn't leave the room or hardly even the bed. All I did was sleep. I loved the tranquillity that I was swimming in, a calm free of time and place. Two weeks where my "master" didn't miss a chance to check up on his merchandise: he'd come every morning and stand anxiously, watching Omayma while she dabbed ointment on my wounds or changed my dressings. Him being around became ordinary, a new part of my reality. But then suddenly he stopped coming by, and I hadn't seen him for the past three days. I asked Nurse Omayma, "Didn't you see the slave trader today?"

"No."

"Isn't it strange? He hasn't come for some time."

"He must be mad at Muallim Ishaq because he asked to buy you before you get sold at the market."

I let out a whoop of joy, not really knowing why. "Really? Will Muallim buy me from him?"

"No, he won't, the slave trader refused."

Omayma removed the cast from my arm and applied some pressure. Then she added, "Don't move your arm for a few more days, and it should heal after ten more. Now get up and walk a little, you've barely left the bed." She pointed to the window.

"You haven't even gone out to the Bimaristan garden. Some fresh air will do you good." Having said that, she made her way to the arched open window that looked out over the garden. Getting out of bed was very difficult for me, almost impossible actually. I lay down and pulled up the white sheet, escaping her chatter. She kept on, "Who can turn down neem flowers!"

"What is she going on about?" I mumbled to myself. "Neem trees only grow in..." I didn't feel myself standing until I was next to Omayma at the window searching for the neem tree that I'd read so much about, and that only grows in India. I felt alive for the first time in the past two weeks, breathing in the air wafting into the room before letting out an exclamation that travelled the length of the vast green garden before my eyes. I'd never in my life seen so many trees, flowers, and plants. Willow, neem, anise, marjoram, sage. I found myself before a paradise of countless medicinal plants, some that I knew of, and others I didn't.

"Oh God, it's so beautiful! How did I miss this?"

"Your master brought you here while you were unconscious, and you were rambling on about Al-Aasefi."

I stayed quiet.

She knew I didn't remember much of what happened.

"When you arrived here, your face was caked in blood, and your clothes torn. Your left arm was broken, and you were hanging on by a thread. The slave trader said that some servant had sold you to him. Was it Al-Aasefi's servant?"

I got lost in my thoughts. That name ate away at me deep inside and stirred up yesterday, doubling the ache in my arm. But the pain buried in the graves of my family was even more unbearable. Al-Aasefi was my father's friend, his brother. He had carted my brothers around on his back, making us a promise of safety when Al-Rashid announced there was no safe place for the Baramika. But Al-Aasefi had suddenly turned on my father and his name kept coming up every time my parents fought. If only Al-Aasefi had just cut off that friendship and backed away, like the others. He had promised my father that he wouldn't betray him.

A promise is a crime if you don't uphold it, a promise is shameful if you break it. He had put his palms on my father's shoulders to comfort him, those safe palms that spilled Baba's blood, and turned me inside out, leaving me to drown in my grief. Did my father make a mistake in trusting him? Being so trusting was my father's biggest downfall. Betrayal sleeps below the shade of trust—if we cut off the branches of this trust, if we uprooted the tree entirely, then we wouldn't be afraid anymore of this treachery that lies sleeping beneath it, waiting for us to take one wrong step: without trust we're safe.

I put on my slippers and braided my brown hair, then went out to the garden, impatient. The Baghdad sun beats

39

down shamelessly, but this place seemed as if it were a piece of paradise: good weather, sweet air, trees along the paved path, standing tall, peacefully embracing each other, flowers and plants of all kinds and colours. In my hands I squeezed the leaves of a fern and inhaled its aroma. I couldn't believe I was missing my pens and paper with me in a place like this bursting with all types of medicinal plants. The word "missing" woke the sadness in my heart. My whole family was in the dirt. I opened my fist and let go of those leaves. I watched them tremble with joy when I did not pull them off.

I saw a group of boys running, they were about the age of my brothers. Curiosity carried my feet, or maybe it was out of habit. I was used to following Rohan and Laween, sticking my nose in all of their business. I sped up in the direction of the great hall, which was crowded with men, their necks stretched out towards a feeble voice. Light flooded the enormous room and my gaze rose to the tallest ceiling I had ever seen. If it wasn't so early, I would have thought that they were getting ready for prayer, all of them quiet, calmly in a circle round this voice.

"...and because farming is the oldest of jobs known to man, plants in all their different forms were God's message to us. We are of the land and for it. Look at the similarities between the human form and plants. Take a moment to think about God's messages ..."

Muallim Ishaq brought together his thumb and forefinger for emphasis, and continued, "Almonds to cure ailments of the head, lemons for the heart, neem leaves for pain in your hands...Everything that we've just mentioned, its shape and composition is like that of the body part if we look carefully and observe. Every herb and plant has its own unique effect you must take note of, because the more time you spend with a patient, the more prepared you will be to create the unique remedy for their specific ailment. How you choose the correct herb will depend on what you observe. You doctors are the heir to this age-old vocation, you're the divine secret that has been preserved for thousands of years on the papyrus of Ancient Egypt. Osiris, Isis, Thoth..."

I had managed to make my way to near the front of the gathering. Muallim Ishaq was seated on a large, throne-like wooden chair. His small body sunk into the deep blue silk cushion, his upper body leaning forward, his beady eyes wandering over those in the crowd. He watched the heads of those around him following his every move and how his words fell on their ears, like pearls not to be wasted. When his eyes fell on me, he straightened up and closed the book that was in his hands. He kept speaking without shifting his gaze from me.

"As it says in the Ebers papyrus, 'I ask you, O Isis, to grant me healing as you healed Horus...'"

He clapped his palm on his forehead and muttered, "What are you saying Ishaq? What comes next?"

"As you healed Horus of all the wounds his brother Set had inflicted on him." The words slipped out of my lips with me even realising it. They scattered inside the large hall clattering loudly, capturing the attention of those present.

I just repeated the sentence that I had learnt by heart from my father's books translated from Greek, without realizing that my voice would be heard in the entire hall. All eyes turned to me searching for the person who had disturbed the peace of this almost holy session. I took a few steps back and lowered my head to avoid the stinging stares.

Muallim Ishaq nodded his head. "Yes, as you healed Horus of all the wounds his brother Set had inflicted on him," he said, his eyes still on me from a distance.

I felt a hand pull at my arm and drag me out of the great hall. I tried not to fall over. Someone barked, "What are you doing?"

"Sorry, but the words just slipped out. I memorise what I read, and I say what I've memorised."

"Professor Ishaq doesn't like anyone interrupting him. Don't you know how difficult it is to get that man to speak? Don't you?"

What makes this old man with his red beard different to the rest? And why was it so hard to get him to speak? There were so many doctors in the medical school, with even more students receiving their training. Yes, he was famous and had a good reputation, but it didn't give him the right keep all the knowledge to himself. Flocks of people started leaving the hall, passing by me and whispering. The man asked one of them, "What happened?"

"He ended the lesson."

The man turned to me, "It'd be better for you to keep your mouth shut."

I looked at the hall. People were restless after my interruption of their lesson. I finally saw Professor Ishaq leave carrying his book in one hand, rubbing his long red beard with the other. I tried to hide but his steps were quicker than my frail walk. He stood directly in front of me. The other man started to apologise, "I'll take her back to her room right away."

Muallim Ishaq didn't pay any attention to him and gestured to me to follow him. He walked in front of me for a while without uttering a word. *Who would ever believe that I was here with Muallim Ishaq?* I glanced at the book in his hand, it was about medicine from the time of the pharaohs. I liked the book itself just as much as the golden ring with the precious blue stone on his index finger, a ring that was as strange as the man before me. I followed him through the large courtyard. He then sat on a seat and asked me, "Are you Hazeer's daughter?"

"Yes."

His eyebrows jumped. He stared at me for a long time. "Wonders never cease in this world, do they?"

I didn't understand what he was getting at, so I kept quiet. He carried on, "Al-Aasefi was your father's friend."

"Friends don't kill each other. I saw his servant stealing everything from our home, even one of my father's manuscripts…"

Muallim Ishaq got up from his place and came closer to me. "Which manuscript?"

I wasn't sure of what I had seen in that manuscript, or what I had heard from my father about it, so I kept quiet. He added, "Did you see what was written on it?"

"I just remember it wasn't in Arabic."

"You can't read Syriac?"

"No. Maybe you can teach me?" I said this shyly because I knew that this man didn't give any student private lessons. My brothers had always dreamt of this, but my father convinced them both that Muallim Ishaq only gave general classes to everyone, and that he didn't teach one-to-one. What chance did a slave like me have? I'll never forget his expression as long as I live—his face lit up, as if he had stumbled across something he had lost. He sat back down and told me to return to my room. His eyes remained focused on the ground as he went back to stroking his long red beard.

Chapter 6

There I was, completely healed. I sat on the edge of the bed looking at the door to my room. I waited for my "master" to come, but he was late. Rather than feeling relieved about it, it made the bad feeling I already had balloon. Death is better than humiliation in life, that's if you even used to own your life. I'd completely surrendered to my fate, it was inescapable. What could a twelve-year-old girl possibly do? Yesterday I had been the daughter of honourable people, and today I was being sold and bought. Soon it was the middle of the afternoon, and the slave trader still hadn't shown up. Nurse Omayma came running to me, clearly on cloud nine. "Muallim Ishaq is calling you to his house!"

"What about the slave trader?"

"Didn't you hear? He's dead!"

It was a stone two-storey building, a small blue door right in the middle of the front of it. I wondered *How can anyone fit through such a small door?* All the doors looked the same: dark blue and small. In front of the door a small dog barked as soon as it saw me. I jumped. I wasn't used to dogs in our home, because Baba didn't want to have to train them. But the dog settled down when it saw its master, Muallim Ishaq. On the way here, the nurse had explained to me how Muallim Ishaq had bought me from the slave trader's son, who had found his father dead on his bedroom floor. She said Muallim Ishaq had taken pity on Hazeer's only surviving child, as my father had been respected by all who worked in Bimaristan, and that's what probably pushed him to buy me. How lucky I was that the greedy slave trader was dead, otherwise right now I'd be being sold in a market to the highest bidder. Muallim Ishaq opened up his arms, "Here you are...welcome."

"Thank you master."

The teacher waved his hand saying, "You're not a slave here. Think of me as your father, girl."

Nurse Omayma said goodbye to me with a peck on my forehead and left. Then my new host guided me to my room.

"I live here alone," he explained. "Since my wife died and my son got married, it's quite quiet."

"You must get lonely."

"Lonely? Being alone isn't as bad as people think it is. The true birth of a person isn't when they come out from the womb into the world, but rather when they leave the world behind to look inwards, and that only happens when you're alone."

46

He turned to me to make sure that I'd understood, but I just looked at him baffled. Even though his beady eyes made me feel something like dread, his words were full of magic, and made me stand still. Muallim gestured to his right at the end of the hallway.

"This is your room. Put your things here and keep them in order." He said this before noticing that my hands were empty. "Not to worry, tomorrow you'll go to the market and buy what you need. You probably won't find me here in the morning because I'll be at Bimaristan." He put a few coins on the table next to the tray of simple food, and then left, closing the door. How good God was. That after everything, I hadn't been left alone, but instead He sent me to this man who rescued me from an inevitable fate. I was so homesick. I missed the Baghdad air; nothing could fill your chest like it. But more important than that, I was closer than I'd ever been to my dream: Bimaristan.

The first threads of sunshine touched my face. The house was quiet, nothing moving inside—I remembered what Muallim Ishaq had said. I wasn't used to such quiet, I was born in a home bursting with the sounds of life. Such silence left me uneasy, so I made my way outside clutching the coins, heading for the market. I was set on buying some clothes because all I had were the ones I was wearing, but then I found myself in front of some bookstores. I'd never been inside one before, though my brothers would always be going to them, coming back

47

with whichever books they wanted. I spent hours browsing one bookstore after another, until I'd spent all my money.

I stood a few steps away from the house, hugging the books to myself, my eyes on the door. The sun had nearly gone down, and I was still standing outside, not daring to go inside. I looked at the dog. He looked at me. Maybe he was wondering what my deal was.

"Books!" Muallim Ishaq surprised me with his weak voice, stretching his neck over my shoulder to get a better look.

"I got them at half price," I babbled. "I couldn't just leave them there."

His eyebrows wiggled up and down. He then gently prised the books from me and took the lead inside the house. He placed the books on the little table in the hallway and gestured for me to follow up him upstairs. We stopped at a worn-down door. He took out a key from his gown pocket and opened the door. I inhaled sharply. There were books piled up, pressed together and others placed in any which way, blanketed with dust. Silver bowls of all sizes were filled with varied herbs. There were different coloured bottles, a white beautiful mortar, and a copper incense burner—my father used to own one just like it. "All of this is yours?" I exclaimed.

I nearly stepped inside when a sharp look from him made me stay where I was just at the threshold. He picked up the copper incense burner and placed it further away. "If you need a book, then just ask for it. But don't ever come in here. Is that understood?" He handed me a book. "Once you finish it, I'll give you another. But…" He fell silent for a moment. Then said, more resolutely, "But don't come in here without my permission." I nodded my head solemnly. "We'll have dinner then you can read it."

⌒

For the first time since my family had been murdered, I was alone with a book. Me, the book, and the lamp. Touching the cover, I felt my father's cracked hands, coarse from pounding so many herbs and stitching up wounds. I passed my hand over the pages before I read it. A powerful homesickness flooded through me, shaking the sea of sorrows inside. My eyes welled up. I closed them tightly so that the tears wouldn't fall. I promised myself that I wouldn't cry until the day I killed Al-Aasefi. An hour passed and then another. I just kept reading.

The next morning when I returned the book to Muallim Ishaq as he was preparing to leave, he looked at me suspiciously. "You read all of it?"

"Yes. And…I want another."

He placed his cloak to the side and asked me to sit down. "Did you used to read all of your father's books?"

"My father would come home with some medical manuscripts, translate them into Arabic, and then ask me to memorise what was in them."

"Do these books have something to do with you wanting to kill Al-Aasefi?" He looked at me intently.

The cat got my tongue. His question was so direct, put so simply. I didn't know if Al-Aasefi was Muallim Ishaq's friend or not. I felt so unprotected in front of Muallim. It was his eyes again, they didn't seem human to me, seeing what most didn't, piercing through my thoughts, tearing down walls, leaving me unarmed, surrendering to them. Some people have the knack of seeing your soul free from all the lies that are buried around it. When you look into their eyes, their souls march into you, and occupy every corner of you, crushing everything in its way and all you can do is submit. They have a strange power that leaves you in chains walking behind them with your head lowered. That's what happened that day when Muallim asked me his question.

"Why so quiet? Everyone heard you scream that day with the nurse." He took the book from me and added, "If you walk among people mourning your family and threatening Al-Aasefi, nothing will come of it except people chasing you. Al-Aasefi is the doctor to Al-Fadl Bin Al-Rabee, the custodian of the caliph. It won't take much for Al-Aasefi to kill you, or imprison you, or sell you as a slave. Nothing destroys a person like their tongue. As for silence, if you're wise enough to be silent, you will have a long, healthy life."

A ball of fire seared my throat, his words stirring up tears that I thought I could keep in. I wanted to cry, but where was Baba? I'd always felt safe in his arms. The night my family died something in me broke. Its shards keep scratching at my soul, leaving me to bleed a little each day. I couldn't keep this anger in anymore, it had become a beast I was unable to tame. If only I could bury the rising waves of this pain...I was drowning. "What good is a long life without them?" I muttered.

Muallim Ishaq straightened up standing and addressed me decisively. "If you want to get rid of your enemies, you've got to live long enough to do so. And for you to survive, you must keep your sorrows to yourself, deep within. You won't reach Al-Aasefi unless you increase your knowledge and resourcefulness."

Part II

Chapter 7

Over the next four years, the closer I got to turning sixteen, the more Muallim Ishaq didn't like to see me cry. He probably thought it made me weak. I never saw him as angry as he was when I cried. Maybe he saw something in my childish face that revealed every single thing I was thinking. He was impressed by my quick intuition, my natural intelligence and just how much I knew—but he didn't trust me for a day.

"Your face always gives you away". I'd always thought that the moment you reveal your sorrows to others, is when you lose your right to be sad. Muallim Ishaq would say, "No matter how bad the pain, bury it, bury it deep. Pain was created to be buried. Let it go as deep as possible to melt, dissolve, and flow through your veins. Pain is what keeps us alive when you think about it." My teacher taught me to boil inside like a volcano without my sky losing its peaceful clouds.

"I want you to accompany me to Bimaristan."

"Me?"

"Al-Aasefi is very close to Gabriel, the head of Bimaristan. Gabriel sent Al-Aasefi to Yemen on a mission, but he'll be back. When the time comes you've got to be completely ready."

"I'm ready, teacher."

"Hardly. You're far from ready. Books may have elevated you above others, but you're still human and need to learn how to exist with them. So, it's necessary to sometimes close the books and look around you, look at faces and learn how to draw from them what will help you live among them. Don't get too involved with them. Keep a fine line between you and them; you'll need it one day."

***

He told me that day about a famous Greek legend. He said I was like the young boy in it, a boy full of himself, proud of his beauty and intelligence. So much so the gods punished him while he was looking at himself in the water, admiring himself. They turned him into a flower.

"If you look closely, you'll see it's a flower that always grows away from other flowers. That's because originally it was the arrogant young boy who didn't like to mix with others. It's the narcissus flower, and you're very much like it Nardeen. When you learn the consequence of arrogance, then I'll take you with me."

***

I thought that Muallim Ishaq had told me the story as a joke, and that he'd obviously take me with him the next day, but some days passed, and then months, and I still had never set foot in Bimaristan. All I'd do was read books and look after the house and dog. I picked up a new habit, which was telling my teacher about all that I'd seen and heard that day.

"Sayyida Aidiya saw me sweeping in front of the house and got upset."

"What day is it today?"

"Saturday…"

He looked at me and repeated, "Saturday, Nardeen."

I must have broken one of the Jewish rules again. Sayyida Aidiya was our neighbour, a rude woman, who was always watching me, scolding me for whatever I did, maybe because she knew that I wasn't Jewish, and that I didn't follow their teachings. But she would get more bothered that Muallim Ishaq let me be free most of the time, as I always had.

With spittle flying from her mouth, she'd seethed, "I saw her with my own two eyes Sayyid Ishaq, I saw her feeding the young boy camel meat. Fine for her to eat it, she's Muslim, but she shouldn't go round tainting our children with those detestable habits."

"What a mischievous girl—how could she do such a thing?" Muallim Ishaq shook his head with what looked like regret. "I'll make sure it doesn't happen again," he would say.

"Sayyid Ishaq, you've got to train your slave girl, otherwise I'll have to beat her."

"Yes, yes, I've heard you Miss Aidiya."

57

I was behind the slightly open front door eavesdropping, occasionally peeking through the crack to look at them both. When Muallim Ishaq came in, I tried to defend myself saying I didn't know about the rule. He stood listening to me make excuses then said calmly, "Don't give anyone what you're eating."

And with that, he went up to his room. I expected him to yell at me, but he didn't. For the first year I lived with him, I slowly learnt the Jewish customs and traditions, and was always fighting with Sayyida Aidiya for one reason or another. But he never blew up at me. All he'd say whenever one of the neighbours complained, "Do that in the house," or "Don't do that outside."

As the days passed, I understood why the narcissus flower dies quickly: it's all alone and can't face the wind, so it gets plucked easily. As for the rest of the flowers, they protect one another, giving each other the power to survive. I didn't want anyone to pluck me out of here, so I started to learn how to go along with Jewish teachings and avoid stepping on anyone's toes. I didn't give up learning from books, but I started to observe the people around me, and learn just as much. Even Sayyida Aidiya stopped complaining about me. One night, Muallim Ishaq opened the door and found her standing outside, grinning from ear to ear. "Is Nardeen in?'

"Yes."

"She promised me that she'd make me some more cough mixture. It really helped me yesterday, I was finally able to sleep in peace."

Muallim Ishaq turned round to me, his eyebrows raised. He watched me as I gave her some more medicine, instructed her to drink it only before bed, and wished her a speedy recovery. After she left he asked, "You used to hate her. What changed?"

"I still do, she's a gossip and sticks her nose in everything, but now I need her."

That night he stood outside my door and stared at me crushing seeds, putting them in silver bowls.

"You're a quick learner Nardeen. I see you're finally listening and trying to change your ways. Hazeer was lucky to have a daughter like you. I wasn't so lucky with my son who ran away."

He paused a long moment. Then he added, "Now you're ready to join me on a trip to Bimaristan."

Chapter 8

The next morning, I got ready to realize my lifelong dream at last. I took off the anklet my mother had given me, but I kept her ring on my index finger. I knew she wouldn't approve me going to Bimaristan, but she'd forgive me as usual. A mother's heart chokes if it keeps its love inside too long.

I tossed my brown plait behind my back and felt my mother stroking it. I focused on choosing the best black scarf I had and tied it round my head. I didn't want a Baramika daughter to seem like she had no morals, my mother wouldn't forgive me for that.

Seeing nurse Omayma again made me feel light. She hugged me firmly.

"It's nice to see you again," she said. She turned to Muallim Ishaq and added, "Have you heard, professor? The guards of the murdered commander say that they didn't hear or see a thing!"

"How unfortunate," he responded, with little concern.

Muallim Ishaq requested that she show me around so that I'd get to know the place. Bimaristan had two sections: one for men, and one for women. The doctors were male, and there were a lot of them. The nurses were female and there were not as many. It seemed that they didn't know as much, so they always needed the supervision of a doctor whenever it was difficult for them to treat a patient.

"But I don't want you to be a nurse," said Muallim Ishaq as he walked in front of me. "I want you to be a doctor who takes on the men here. I don't want you to just be as good as them, I want you to shake them up. The knowledge that you possess surpasses that of all the new students."

My teacher had faith that I could be a star here. I had memorised all those books and manuscripts, and all I was missing was the practical application of what I had learnt. My first duty was to help Muallim Ishaq with whatever he needed, and then to learn. I wasn't meant to touch a patient without his permission or treat one without consulting him. I was here as his student, to follow his commands and only answer to him. I wasn't able to do whatever I pleased, because I was meant to be his shadow. If he moved, I moved. If he was still, I was still. It was a small price to pay I thought if I was on my way to becoming like him: strong, respected. I was on my journey for the everlasting glory that my father never got even though he did so many good deeds.

"What if people ask me my name?" That's all I was worried about. No one in Bimaristan had forgotten the accusation that the Baramika had poisoned Harun Al-Rashid's cousin, and even if tongues had stopped wagging about it, the hearts of people who had loved Musa Bin Ja'far wouldn't have forgotten. Especially not when his murder was followed by the discovery of other dead officials in the kingdom the same morning. No one had seen or heard anything —no screams or commotion of any sort. Even their guards swore it had been a clear night. Since the guards hadn't seen anyone, everyone assumed the murderer must have been a demon.

The idea of people thinking I was the daughter of a demon who slipped into houses and stole the souls of men, leaving without anyone ever seeing him—terrified me. I was afraid to see the hatred in their eyes. Living here was a dream, but I was like a moth drawn to the flame—would the Bimaristan burn me? My legs froze. I was stuck in place. I asked him, "What if they know that the demon's daughter is still alive? What if they kill me like they killed him?"

Muallim Ishaq came close to me and shook me hard.

"Demons don't die. If your father had been one, he'd still be alive. You have a chance to live Nardeen, at least don't die as easily as your father did."

On this earth, it wasn't enough to be smart. Being smart can get you into all kinds of trouble that being stupid won't. You've got to be strong to protect your intelligence, you've got to discover secret escape routes for yourself to guarantee your safety in case someone wants you dead. Especially if they have the desire to do so and the ability to kill you as well.

What does the caliph want with all those bright men and scholars he surrounds himself with? To make him immortal while they work as hard as they do for the sake of knowledge? What do they want in return? Money? Power? Some of them, or a lot of them, are hoping to just stay alive when chaos breaks out, to be in the only lifeboat when the ship sinks. My father wasn't one of them. He thought that loving the poor and the homeless was more important. Politics was never a priority for him. What does a person gain if they surround themselves with weak people? A strong enemy will push you further ahead than a hundred weak friends, that's what my teacher believed, and that's what I've also grown to believe.

I went along with my teacher to Bimaristan on Sundays, Mondays, and Tuesdays to examine his patients in the morning. I observed and learned, sometimes helping him when the situation called for it. As for the rest of the week, he would move from ministers' palaces to those of even higher up leaders, following up on the condition of an old sheikh whose life had drained from his sickly body until you could almost be certain he was dead. Or he'd inspect someone's sword wound from some battle or another endless war. All of these men were in charge of something; they had influence. They were nothing like my father's patients. My father was a skilled doctor, but Muallim Ishaq was more than a doctor, he was a legend in medicine. I had never seen a man as calm as him in the face of death.

We were in one of the rich people's homes. Muallim Ishaq placed his hand on the gaunt sheikh's neck, then shook his head as a sign that he had died. Those standing in attendance muttered their condolences, "*La hawla wa la quwata illa billah.*" There is no power or strength save in God.

In that moment, a woman burst in wailing, screaming, "Ali! My son, Ali!" She was a servant in the home. She grabbed my teacher by the collar and pleaded with him to take a look at her son who had been bitten by a snake, but my teacher responded he was only there to treat the master of the house. She was desperate, her voice trembling, panicked. Her weary eyes tore at my heart. I didn't know how I slipped out right then, but I followed the woman to her son's room. He was spread out on the mattress. He looked no more than seven years old, his eyes staring into space. His face was blue, his body shuddering as if it were a feather a strong wind was playing with. I stared at his swollen leg and tried to inspect it, but his yelps made me even more flustered, so I just stayed, standing staring into his little face twisted in pain. How did I get into this? Muallim Ishaq pushed me to one side and strode towards the boy. Where did he come from? "Pillows, Nardeen!" he snapped.

I propped the pillows behind the boy's back until his chest and head were higher than his legs. Whilst tying a strap around his thigh, and pulling tightly on it, my teacher asked, "Where was he bitten?"

"On the right leg, by his ankle."

"Do you remember what we do next?"

I fell silent for a moment, trying to gather my thoughts. "We keep the heart higher, so that no poison can reach it and then…"

65

"Then?"

He didn't wait for my answer, and pounced on the area where the bite was, opening it with a sharp knife, and sucking out the poison. He spat and then sucked some more. He did this several more times till he was out of breath, then looked at me. "Now?"

"We tie his leg to slow down the spread of the poison, and cut open the area where the bite is…"

My teacher listened to every word I uttered. I wasn't able to read his thoughts. Was he mad at me? He had nodded his head signalling I was correct, and if not for the beads of sweat glistening on his forehead, I would have thought he didn't care about the boy at all. He seemed so relaxed while he was shooting questions at me, and getting on with his work, as if he was in charge of the life that was slipping through our fingers—that it wouldn't end without his say-so. I was worried about the boy, but Muallim Ishaq seemed more concerned about how much I knew. We both were in the presence of death, but I was just a student while he was the teacher. Finally, he put a Dodonaea poultice on the wound and instructed me to stay by the patient's side. "You'll spend the night here, the boy is in your care. Fever, nausea, and intense thirst are all symptoms that you'll see in the next few hours. Are you ready?"

He wanted me to stay? I thought he'd tell me off because I had disobeyed him by treating this boy. Sure, I had been by his side for the past year at Bimaristan and the houses of dignitaries in Baghdad, but me, staying alone to take care of a patient seemed risky. Was this his way of punishing me?

How could a fourteen-year-old girl take care of a boy on the verge of death? If fever took hold of his body, then he'd die in my arms tonight. I didn't have what it would take to make it through this. My hands started to tremble, my mind racing. My teacher came closer and squeezed my cold hands. He whispered firmly, "Don't tremble, you're the one who decided to help him. Finish what you started."

"I'm scared."

"It doesn't matter what you feel. What counts is that you show up when the door opens, and that people see before them a doctor. If you don't believe in yourself, no one else ever will."

Chapter 9

It was the first time I saved a life. The fever went down, and the boy stopped vomiting. I made him drink a lot of water till his body rejected whatever was left of the poison. I'll never forget his mother's joy—her eyes wide and glowing. She looked at me with pride while my teacher's expression was pinched.

He didn't speak to me for a week. I knew I had made a mistake when I broke his rules for a second time, after already having tried to get into his library to get his copper incense burner.

"I already told you, Nardeen. Don't come in this room without me."

"I just wanted to borrow the incense burner…"

"It's not to be touched. Do you understand me?"

It was tough for me to draw the line between what upset him and what didn't upset him. He got angry when I had tried to borrow the incense burner, but he didn't move a muscle when I went against the Jewish teachings. I wanted to remain close to a man of his reputation. I wanted to learn from him. And so, that's how Ishaq the Jew was never seen without Nardeen the Baramika—a bow and arrow, a reed pen and its inkwell, that's how we both were.

Someone came to us before one of his lessons, while I was writing down what my teacher was dictating. "Aren't you taking this a bit too far, Muallim Ishaq?" he said sharply. "Since when do nurses attend lectures with us men?"

"This girl isn't a nurse. She's my student and my assistant. None of you can match her skills in Syriac, and you yourself haven't read all the books that she has. If you want, stay, otherwise go—it's not appropriate for someone like you to be sitting with the likes of her anyways."

That's how my teacher thought of me…as a daughter. It made me think, do we choose our own path or does the path choose us? Do we walk on it leaving behind fresh footprints or do we follow a trail that's already laid out for us? Did I want to be in Bimaristan so much that I fought to stay alive that dark night? Or was it that the Bimaristan wanted me so much, that it removed all obstacles from a Baramika girl

70

entering, even if her family had to die in the process? Here I was after three years of work in Bimaristan, more than a nurse but less than a doctor. I was what no other woman in Baghdad has been before: Nardeen the Baramika, the teacher's daughter, spawn of a demon. I was okay with this last label too, because so many problems evaporated, afraid of this nickname. It's okay for you to lose everything, even your family and your reputation. That's what my teacher said. "Loss is a good thing."

"What's so great about loss, Muallim?"

"You no longer have what you used to worry about."

He made me realise that everything that awakens uncertainty in us and handcuffs our hopes, and puts limits on us, is fear. Fear over what we own, over ourselves, our family, our reputation, our health. Loss saves us the trouble of looking back. All that is behind us is destruction, and what's to come won't be worse than what we left behind. When you lose everything, you have nothing left to lose, and so you're a winner.

Bimaristan had become my safe place. I found peace in it from the faded memories that still cast their shadow over everything I do. These memories still walk in step with me down the corridors, coming loose with every last breath I witness, raising its head among the groans of the tortured patients. I search in the eyes of those leaving this world for my father's fear that night. I search in the air of their rooms for that sweet smell from my family's last night. The smell of death here isn't anything like what I smelled that night. It seems Death chose only us to inhale a whiff of its real fragrance.

～

Often, we're not aware of just how deep the crack runs that leaves us in two, scattered, our soul torn between a lover's heart and a feverish, brilliant brain. We turn miserable, chased down by the curse of choice. Which one will you choose? Mind or heart, you'll only ever be half satisfied, half-happy, half alive.

"Can I read your notes from Muallim's lecture?"

His sunny voice lit something inside of me. I turned quickly to see who was speaking and was met with a smile. He pointed to the papers in front of me.

～

The men who attended my teacher's lectures weren't exactly happy to have me around. I was always on his right, with my pen, recording what he said. Some of them looked at me with slitted eyes, while others expressed their displeasure out loud to my Muallim. But no one had ever spoken to me, maybe they felt it would make them look less of a man. During my three years here at Bimaristan, no one had succeeded in convincing Muallim Ishaq to make me leave. He'd always respond, "If she goes, I go," and no one was prepared to lose out on his lectures. I became like his shadow, always around. But here was this boy not only talking to me, but looking at me directly, grinning. I had been quiet for too long. Again, he spoke first.

"Would Muallim Ishaq be against me seeing them?"

"Yes…you're right." I folded the pages up and hurried to make my way out of the hall. My pace increased, my brisk walk breaking out in a run. Why was I running? I slowed down and caught my breath. I checked the papers to make sure I hadn't left any behind. They were all in my hand. But why did I keep feeling like I'd left something behind? His smile came back to me, but when I turned back towards the hall, he was nowhere to be seen. I wondered what he'd be thinking now. Probably what everyone else did, "Muallim Ishaq's girl is just like him, so rough, so heartless." But if that were true, then what was beating so hard in my chest?'

Was it a long night or was it just my thoughts that had made time stop? I didn't know. My head felt like it was splitting in two. That's all I got out of that night. Even the cheerful morning that draped the large hall in a new outfit, chasing away its usual sameness, couldn't chase away my headache. But seeing his face there at the end of the hall, took all the hurt away.

I caught sight of him in one of the back corners, his arms folded across his chest, hanging onto every word Muallim was saying. He could have come closer because there was a space up front, but he seemed more comfortable in that corner of his. It wasn't long though before he made his way towards the entrance. My eyes trailed him. As he left without even turning round to look at me, I felt my heart flutter.

Chapter 10

Finally, the skies in Baghdad showered us with rain. Autumn was just starting; the furious sun that had roasted the tops of people's heads grew tired and faded away, hiding behind a veil of clouds. The trees shrugged off the joy of summer, blanketing the ground with blossoms that had given up, but not without first filling the courtyard with the last of what they possessed: a sweet-smelling fragrance.

My teacher sat squarely on his chair and pointed to me. I held out his book to him. The place was crowded: students, doctors, and other just curious individuals. This was the last time he'd be giving a lecture before he took off for some days.

At around this time of year, he would take a break from work. He'd carry some supplies, very little money, and tell me to take care of myself and the house until he returned. Each time, one of the dogs accompanied him. The dog would go with him, and never come back. Over the past four years I've counted four dogs that have disappeared. Maybe my teacher was like stone when it comes to feeling anything for them when they died, but I always cried over them, even if I didn't do it in front of him.

He cleared his throat momentarily and everyone grew quiet. "For the ancient Egyptians, medicine was like magic, that's to say that priests took advantage of their knowledge to convince the sick of whatever they wanted. They fooled the sick into thinking that the illnesses which afflicted their bodies were evil spirits, and that the concoctions that these priests made contained the essence of the gods. So more of the sick started looking for their cure in temples…"

I looked at the papers in front of me. Empty and faded. Today everything seems empty, even this hall full of faces of all kinds, feels empty. That boy, if he wanted to hear Muallim's lectures, then why didn't he attend? I looked around the crowd, but he wasn't there…

"Nardeen…Nardeen."

I was drowning in my thoughts when my teacher's voice knocked against my ears. "Yes!" I shouted.

He fixed me with a strange look. "Aren't you writing anything down?"

"Of course…" I picked up my quill and made it look like I was writing. I tried to focus on every single word he was saying, but it didn't take long for me to slip once more into my maze of thoughts. I wasn't aware of anything he said. My teacher got up from his seat, and I too got ready to stand. He turned to me.

"I'll go home before you. Make sure you return the books to the Bimaristan library." He paused. "Do you understand what I've just said?"

I nodded quickly, and he left. I stayed in the hall trying to organise what I had written, and checking which books had to be given back. While looking at the bird's nest of jumbled sentences I'd written in the few moments I'd forced my mind to focus, I exhaled. The blank spaces pointed to how distracted I had been from what he was saying. O God, how could I have blanked out so terribly on today's lesson? Medicine for the ancient Egyptians was a topic that only very few doctors grasped, and Muallim Ishaq alone possessed all of this knowledge, and here I had been absent-minded, not having written anything worth reading.

I walked, dragging my legs, putting myself down even more. I set the books back where they belonged and then walked to the patients' rooms. One of the nurses chased me, panting.

"Nardeen! I need you."

I followed her to the last room on the corridor. We stopped in front of a bone-thin man who could barely catch his breath between coughs.

"I know that Muallim Ishaq only likes you to treat his patients, but this man just came to us yesterday with this horrible cough. None of the medicines I've given him have helped."

My teacher had always forbidden me from touching any patient that he wasn't already treating, usually rich people or

cases that I could learn something new from. If he found out
that I treated someone without his permission, he'd lose it. I
turned this all over in my head, again and again. Why couldn't
I just be more standoffish like Muallim Ishaq? Why did I
always see Baba's face in the faces of these desperate patients?
I thought of refusing, but the man's breathing was weak, and
his faint moaning was heart-breaking…

"Nardeen?" The nurse sensed I wasn't going to help her.

I looked at the man again, and knew that if I didn't
speak, then everyone in this room would die and maybe the
nurse too. "Who's the doctor in charge here?" I asked. "This
man has pneumonia and shouldn't be mixing with the other
patients."

The nurse staggered a few steps back and placed her hand
over her nose.

I repeated my question. "Who's in charge of him and the
others?"

"I am."

My eyes grew wide, and I felt my heart beating in my
ears when he appeared before me, upright, tall. He entered
the room, greeted the nurse with a fleeting smile and then
grew serious. He didn't look at me. Instead, he went directly
to the man that was barely breathing and lay his hand on his
forehead. "But he doesn't have a fever. How do you know its
pneumonia?"

I wiped my sweaty palms on my thawb and took the man's
fingers in my hand. I pointed to his nails. "Wide and yellow
nails. The Greeks call it Hippocrates fingers, which means
that the sickness is still in the early stages."

I peeked at him and saw him staring at me. I felt my face grow hot. He pulled the patient's hand to him and gave it a hard look. "Hippocrates' fingers? How could I miss that?"

I felt a strange sense of victory watching him confirm what I had just said. He asked the nurse to prepare a separate room for the man. I walked away but heard his steps following me. He kept walking until he overtook me and whipped round to me with the same smile he had the first time I saw him. Curiosity won me over. He couldn't be more than a few years older than me. I asked him, "How does it make sense for you to be a doctor but you're probably not even twenty?"

"Not any more sense than you being a doctor, seeing as you're a girl, but you can't be a nurse either because you know more than them already. If Muallim Ishaq chose you to be by his side then you must be..."

I raised my eyebrows. "You know him?"

"You're not the only one who's been his favourite student..."

Chapter 11

I lay on my bed mulling over what Suhaib had told me. It was rare for Muallim Ishaq to tutor someone privately, and so if he really had been his private student once upon a time, why was he coming to class in secret? And what made their relationship so sour? Suhaib definitely looked up to Muallim, but why didn't he want him to know he's there? His words were hiding something. Every time he stopped speaking, his twitching lips gave him away.

I heard the dog barking and my heart ached. This was the last time that I'd see the animal. Like all the other dogs, he wouldn't come back after this trip. Once I had made my way downstairs, I saw my teacher petting his head. I got closer to them both without him noticing. It was nice to imagine my Muallim as a young child, playing with his dog. Maybe this time his face would show some kind of sadness that I never got to see otherwise, but I knew it was deep down there somewhere. He was like me, grief lived in him. The body may only need time to heal, but the soul needs more than time. The soul needs another one like it to heal, and who knows, it could happen overnight, like me and my teacher's souls. I whispered, "Why don't you leave him behind this time? Isn't he too small for such a journey?"

"I wish I could, but the trip can't happen without him."

We both fell silent, saying our goodbyes to this young dog with our long faces. My teacher whispered, "I saw him today. He's back."

"Who?"

"Al-Aasefi. He came to me here at home."

⁓

I don't know how much time passed while I just stared at my teacher, speechless. The calmness with which he said this all stunned me. Nothing seemed to change in him, whereas all my senses were agitated when I heard that name. I thought that I'd be stronger when we met again, I thought I'd be able to stuff my sorrow down deep, cover it up. But I didn't know that this sorrow had taken root deep inside of me, making it impossible to uproot. It was buried, but not dead, always sucking everything out of me in life, but as my teacher said, it left me with just enough to keep on living.

He cut through the silence saying, "I can't postpone the trip, so you've got to be careful. I don't want you getting close to him. I don't want him knowing you're in Bimaristan. Are we clear Nardeen?"

I didn't answer him, so he placed his hand on my head, and said with some finality, "We'll kill him Nardeen...Just a little patience my girl."

On the days where I went to Bimaristan while he was away, the wild racing of my heart left me confused. Was it Suhaib's words that made me feel alive again or knowing that Al-Aasefi and I shared the same land and sky, breathing in the same air? Was it love or hatred that made my heart feel like it was going to burst? Every time I tried to curl up in my sorrow, every time I tried to grope my way through my memory to that pitch-black night and I inhaled the sweet scent of death that isn't like anything I know, Suhaib's handsome face pulled me back to life, his welcoming boyish grin, so genuine to the point that I felt like running away with him from everything that was and what will be.

We hung around in the gardens after classes or in between taking care of our patients. In the rains, we would huddle in a corner of the Bimaristan, sharing our food and talking about our dreams. My first thoughts in the morning and my last thoughts at night were of Suhaib.

He tilted his head back, bringing his jawline into full view, his sculpted nose, a hint of stubble that I wanted to stroke. His laugh that made him that much more irresistible. One day, with a deep sadness he said, "You're really like him, you've become just like him, Muallim Ishaq."

"And who wouldn't want that?"

I didn't get angry at him for comparing me to my teacher, I was proud of it. In just a few days, the easiness that grew between Suhaib and I made me smile instead. I pictured myself with a black turban on my head and a golden ring with a blue precious stone on my wrinkled finger that would twinkle whenever I was explaining something or the other, me sitting on a chair in the grand hall with students flocking round me, hanging onto my every word. I was delighted to be like my teacher. My cheeks hurt from smiling. Suhaib came closer to me till the distance between us meant I had to look into his eyes. I looked up at the sky instead and felt his eyes on me. I didn't want to seem flustered so I blurted out, "Looks like rain."

"Who needs rain when my heart beats for the clouds in your eyes?"

His words were enough to make joy bloom inside of me, small and weak, but still there. I felt bad for this joy that had to live side by side with my sadness extending its leaves; dark, thick leaves that covered everything and kept both air and light out. How could joy ever grow in the shadow of this poisonous tree? I'd keep worrying over this joy carrying it as delicately as a seed inside me. I couldn't fully free myself of the pain. I wasn't ready to give in to this kind of pure joy while I was still trying to keep my head above my grief. My grief didn't give me the right to be happy like any other young girl with love knocking at her door. It kept reminding me that the Baramika didn't have the right to love anyone, and nobody had to love us. It was enough for us Baramika to have the luxury of staying alive, and it would be enough for me to have the honour of killing the person who gave me this luxury.

Even so, Suhaib and I became inseparable. We studied at the same table in Bimaristan library, sitting close. We walked to classes together. On cold days, he would lay my thick cloak gently over my shoulders. I so wanted to reach out and hold his hand. I would catch him looking at me, and he'd turn the look into a smile; his warm, beautiful smile that would light up the room and make my heart beat like thunder.

Tongues wagged of Al-Aasefi coming back, but no one had seen him in Bimaristan. People said he was the most likely candidate to become Bimaristan's vice chancellor. The Caliph's vizier had promised to help him get that position after coming back from Yemen. But since he hadn't been to the school yet, even though he was in Baghdad, many wondered why. Now, whenever I set foot in Bimaristan, I felt a wave come over me, where all I could think about was getting to see Al-Aasefi's face, asking him, "Why? Why did you kill my father?" I wanted him to give me a straight answer. No need to complicate things, no political conspiracies, or uncertain rumours. What good was an answer if it just led to more questions? It was a terrifying cycle that I couldn't bear staying in for one more day.

Chapter 12

I stood under Bimaristan's stone-vaulted entrance, keeping out of the rain that started to pour down in the early hours of the evening. Suhaib promised me that he'd see me before I left school that day, so where was he now? I stretched my hand out under the shower of drops, listening to their light pattering on my palm. It stirred in me some kind of comfort and calm. From a distance, I saw his silhouette hurrying towards me. I pulled my hand back out of the rain and placed it behind my back, so that he wouldn't think that I was reaching out for him. He stood in front of me, his clothes wet, his chiselled face dripping. He yelled trying to make himself heard over the pouring rain, his smile never leaving his face. "I told you to wait for me inside!"

"If it wasn't raining, I wouldn't still be here."

He knew I was annoyed with him being late. "Don't you feel bad for your beautiful face to be frowning like that? I'm late because I was telling the Bimaristan chancellor that my father will be in school tomorrow."

"Your father knows the chancellor?"

"Yes…"

Suhaib lowered his eyes to the ground for a moment, then said bitterly, "But he's sick now…really sick."

I felt the sadness that flowed over him, extinguishing his glowing smile. Consoling him, I said, "Have faith, God never forgets his servants. He's with you."

"Can I ask you a favour?"

"Of course."

"Can you come in tomorrow? I know you usually stay home when Muallim Ishaq comes back from trips, but I think my father's sickness is really serious and that's why he won't tell anyone about it. When he comes to observe me looking after some patients that I'm treating, I want you to be there tomorrow. I want you to stay next to us so that you can see his symptoms up close. I think I have an idea of what it could be, but I want to be sure. Can you do that?"

"Definitely," I replied without hesitating.

Later, I thought to myself that whenever Suhaib would talk about himself or about Muallim Ishaq, and what he learnt from him, he'd be animated but it would be mixed with something like sadness at being apart from him. But he didn't really talk about his father much. All he told me was that he was a doctor and had a privileged position with Bimaristan's chancellor. Just remembering how he had asked me to help him made me float with happiness. I felt the seed of joy in me grow stronger after having been weakened. It grew and grew, becoming much bigger than I ever deserved.

Early the next morning I reached the patients' room. I took my place next to one of the patients, anticipating Suhaib's and his father's arrival. Two nurses started tidying up the place, making sure each patient had eaten their breakfast. They seemed nervous, trying to make sure everything was where it should be. I thought to myself that Suhaib had never mentioned his father being intimidating. A tall man entered, looking about fifty-something. His black, tired eyes scanned the room. Next to him was Suhaib trying to keep up with wide strides. When he saw me, he beamed, and I grinned back. He tilted his head towards the man next to him, and I understood that it was his father.

I looked intently at them while they worked in harmony: the father would speak and the son would nod his head in agreement. He'd point and his son would bring the necessary medicines and poultices. Then I remembered what Suhaib had asked me to do. So, I started staring at his father to see what kind of illness he was suffering from: gaunt, a slight hunch. He'd talk for a little then fall silent to catch his breath, as if his chest was closing in on itself. His voice was hoarse and his hands trembling. His chest shuddered again, and he hurried to cover his mouth with a handkerchief to hide his sharp cough that everyone in the room heard. It was obvious he had pneumonia.

One of the nurses whispered in the other's year, all the while looking at Suhaib and his father making their way to the door, "Who'd believe that weak old man is Al-Aasefi?"

"He must be really sick."

My heart stopped. I turned to have another look at the man. Suhaib saw my grave expression and flashed me a goofy grin, but I didn't respond. My eyes were fixed on his father. I looked firmly at his face, and his features that looked so much like Suhaib's made my throat tighten: his nose, his eyes, his cheekbones, the colour of his skin, they were spitting images of each other—but Al-Aasefi looked nothing like the image of him I had in my mind. Who would believe that a face like this was the devil himself?

I didn't wait for Suhaib to come back. It was still raining. I walked in the drizzle, my steps faltering. Maybe the sky didn't want to see me cry, so it cried first. The sky was the only one who saw the way I was wailing shrilly inside. When I opened the door, I saw Muallim Ishaq sitting on his wooden chair, wrapped up in his cloak, with a short glass of steaming tea in his hand, keeping him warm on that cold evening. He put it to the side and asked me to come closer. He looked at me his head tilted to the side. "My feet are hurting. Don't make me get up. Come here, Nardeen."

I felt like I had broken my promise to him. That the distance I had worked so hard to bridge between us over the past years, had now widened more than ever. What a horrible feeling. Regret was eating away at me. I knew exactly what

I had done. I took two steps towards him and knelt down. I felt his hand on my head and a cry I had been holding in for so long, came out high and sharp. Worn out from waiting, he asked, "What happened Nardeen? Were you at Bimaristan?"

Where should I begin?

"Did you meet Al-Aasefi?"

I nodded. He grabbed my chin and raised my head up roughly. "Does he know who you are?"

"No, but his son does."

"Which son? Who? Suhaib?"

He wrapped his abaya around me and pulled it tight. Then he went to the teapot and poured me a glass. "Drink this, it's cold tonight."

I told him all about Suhaib without sharing how strongly I felt about him. I wanted this heavy burden to be lighter. I knew that Muallim Ishaq's back was stronger than mine. And that his narrow eyes always had the power to see more than what anyone else could. He looked at the ground, rubbing his gold ring. As usual, he didn't say a word.

Chapter 13

That day all the doctors and nurses were gathered in the large hall with the president of Bimaristan, Sayyid Gabriel, to talk about Harun Al-Rashid's wife Zubeida, and how sick she was. For months she had been suffering from different pains in her body that would grip her sharply for days on end and then suddenly leave her for weeks, as if they had never been there. Then they would come back once again, so she contacted Sayyid Gabriel for a consultation. At the very front were the most important doctors. Suhaib was there, in his turban that highlighted his forehead, making him look more handsome than ever. His father sat next to him. Suhaib's expression communicated his confusion over where I had been for the past few days.

It was probably my walk in the rain that day which had caused the high fever that kept me in bed. My body was trembling from how cold I felt, while my fever rocketed. My head felt like it was about to explode. Not being able to eat anything, I got worse. I was so weak. But Muallim Ishaq insisted that my body was fine and that my heart was the one leading me down this road of destruction. He warned me about the consequences of staying in the middle of the road for too long.

"You've got to make a decision. Are you going to take revenge on Al-Aasefi or not?"

"What's the point? He's going to die anyways."

"So I'm not the only one who noticed. You know he's got pneumonia."

"Well, he had it all under control until now. But he'll be dead any day now."

"Are we just going to sit and wait till he dies, Nardeen? Don't you want to speed it up?"

It wasn't hard for Al-Aasefi to reduce his symptoms. Pneumonia is a sickness that only ends in death, but a doctor like him could ease the symptoms with herbs and medicines available to him. Then it just became a matter of time. As for Muallim Ishaq, he couldn't bear it, having to see Al-Aasefi in front of him still, even though he knew he was dying.

The voices of the doctors grew louder in the hall. Each of them wanted to have the honour of treating Zubeida. The president of Bimaristan stood trying to get a handle on the situation. "Gentlemen!" he yelled. "There's no point choosing one man over the other because you know that her Majesty

94

Zubeida is a pious Hashemite, meaning no man can look upon her even if he is a doctor."

"The nurses can accompany us," someone said loudly. "They can look under her hijab and maybe we'll get to the root of her illness."

Someone else responded, "We've done that before and haven't gotten anywhere. Nurses simply don't look for the same things that doctors do."

"We've got to send someone who has the same attention to detail and depth of knowledge as a doctor does," my teacher said as he walked towards the Bimaristan president. He went on, "Let's send a girl who brings together the qualities of a doctor and a nurse."

It seemed like everyone in the hall knew who he meant, except for me! Me, who just sat staring into my teacher's face, while he pointed me out in the middle of the crowd. He wanted me to go. I swallowed slowly. If I didn't know him, I would have thought he was joking, or just trying to scare me, but my Muallim never joked. Ever since the first time we met four years ago, I had never seen Muallim Ishaq smile. His face was always like stone, empty of any expression, except the slight curl of his lips, or a raised eyebrow if he was surprised. No one could ever be absolutely certain of what he was feeling. Even the words he uttered created the illusion that you understood them, but truly hid more than they revealed. Everyone in the hall had turned to look at me, so I didn't think it would be right for me to keep sitting. I stood, trying to stay calm, my nails digging into my palms. But Muallim

Ishaq didn't take it easy on me and grabbed me by the wrist, leading me to the middle of the hall.

"All of you know that Nardeen isn't like the other nurses. You all have seen how extensive her knowledge is, how sound of mind she is, and the accuracy of her opinion."

I could see Al-Aasefi's face clearly from where I was standing. He leaned towards his son and whispered something in his ear that made Suhaib's jaw tighten and nostrils flare. Al-Aasefi then turned to me and smiled. Balancing himself on his son's shoulder, he got up from where he was.

"A little girl like this treating Her Majesty Zubeida? Isn't there anyone else here better than her?"

"Nardeen is the best student I've ever had," Muallim responded in a low voice, almost like a growl. "She's even better than me in some respects."

Al-Aasefi let out a bark of a laugh that caused his chest to tense up. He started coughing again. Wiping the corner of his mouth with his handkerchief, he commented, "We're not going to send someone to the Caliph's course simply because they're your star student Ishaq." Then he added, "Especially not a girl we hardly know."

"Nardeen isn't a stranger, don't you remember her Al-Aasefi?"

My teacher drew nearer to Al-Aasefi before pronouncing the last words that would leave Al-Aasefi with his mouth hanging open. "How could you forget Nardeen? The daughter of your friend, Hazeer?"

After hearing what my teacher had to say, the hall erupted. People always live in their memories. Forgetting is a temporary thing. Everyone here hadn't forgotten my father

96

being dismissed and falsely accused, all because the murder of Musa Bin Ja'far, the caliph's cousin, happened at the same time my father translated a rare book about poisons. For his enemies, that was more than enough evidence. At that time most people weren't willing to stand with my father. They didn't want to get caught in the middle between the Baramika and the caliph. But today they were convinced that my father was killed unjustly, that he was innocent. They believed that those fanatics who spilled my family's blood wouldn't have dared to do so if the cord of affection between Al-Rashid and the Baramika hadn't been cut. The fact that some powerful men in the kingdom were found murdered under similar circumstances after my father's death, proved that the real killer was still out there.

My blood froze in my veins when I saw Al-Aasefi approach me, his stare throwing sparks. He stood close to me and peered into my face for what felt like forever. He whispered, unbelieving, "Hazeer's daughter? Didn't everyone die that night?"

In the same hushed tones, my Muallim responded, "The only person who could answer you is Nardeen. Do you want to ask her about what she saw that night?"

Al-Aasefi's face grew pale, he nearly collapsed from the sharp coughing that overtook him. Suhaib hurried to his side to steady him. The Bimaristan chancellor got up, irritated by what he saw. "Enough. We won't send anyone till we confirm that she is qualified. And now, I want you two gentlemen to follow me."

The Bimaristan chancellor left with Al-Aasefi and Muallim Ishaq, while the rest of the hall scattered, leaving one after the other. Only Suhaib and I were left, waiting. Each of us looking at the other without saying a word. I felt my hands trembling and laced them together, trying to calm down, and draw patience from somewhere. But Suhaib's patience had run out. "What did Muallim Ishaq say to my father?"

"I don't know."

"Enough with your lies! I know that Muallim Ishaq and my father are competing for the vice chancellor position of this school, but what does that have to do with you?"

I looked into the distance and didn't answer, leaving him to drown in his questions. He'd probably go a little bit crazy, but then he'd come to his senses. So be it. It was better than him hearing all the answers that would end everything between us. I'd rather the both of us die instead of our love dying. This delicate feeling wouldn't be able to carry the weight of the past, it would break. And there's no power that would be able to put it back together again. Our love would be wiped away and disappear under the rivers of blood that were spilled that night. Even though I'd decided to cut my ties with Suhaib, I still wanted him to keep this love of ours in his heart, healthy and alive, unharmed. I wanted him to always smile when he thought of me. It'd be too horrible for him to hear the answers I had. I couldn't leave him with the disgrace of his father being a killer, his heart broken in two.

Al-Aasefi came out of the room first. His eyes were cold and hard. A vein throbbed in his neck. He shot me a dirty look.

Before Suhaib went after him, he turned to me and made sure his father was out of range. "I don't know what you and my father have against each other, but I'll tell you what Nardeen. Don't believe everything Muallim Ishaq tells you. He's not as perfect as you think he is."

Suhaib jogged away, leaving behind a storm of thoughts that almost uprooted me from where I stood. I looked at my teacher who was also out of the room now and making a beeline for me. "Tomorrow you'll be in Al-Rashid's palace."

"But…"

"I don't want to hear a thing from you, we've already agreed on this."

"When?" I exploded. "We never agreed on anything! All I ever wanted was to seek revenge on the man who killed my father. As for going into Al-Rashid's palace, that's a whole other thing."

"Do you think it'll be easy to hurt Al-Aasefi and then go on with your life without his cronies coming back to haunt you? It's the same game that your father refused to play. And that's why he's dead, Nardeen."

Muallim Ishaq was right. It was the same game that my father had refused to play. He had refused to enter Al-Rashid's palace, and for his profession as a doctor to simply become a means to an end. A lot of doctors like him refused to get into politics as they were afraid of the unknown. Only a handful gambled with their lives in this game. And maybe even some of them became good at it like Al-Aasefi, but I didn't care about that anymore. All I cared about in this moment was one thing: "What about you? Do you play the game, Muallim?"

Muallim Ishaq was about to say something, but he clammed up at the last minute, turned on his heel, and left the hall without answering. I must have crossed some kind of line. Maybe so, but I knew that I wouldn't get anything until I crossed such boundaries. Every time I did so, I saw a new side of my teacher. It felt like I never really knew him at all, only seeing him from one angle, and I could never figure out if the new sides I saw were really him or not. What I was sure about is that I'd seen the different faces he wore, which had started to confuse me. I was afraid to look deeper, to really pick him apart. I'd just end up wondering, "Who *is* my Muallim, really?"

Chapter 14

Sleep escaped me. I couldn't close my eyes knowing that I had said something which could have upset my teacher. I came out of my room and found him perched on his chair, wide awake. He was reading a book by the light of a lantern next to him. He looked up at me then went back to reading. I drew closer to him and tried to organise in my head what I should say to him. He surprised me by speaking first. "You're a quick student Nardeen. You grew to be just like me in everything. Everything except your face that always shows what's in your heart. All I can think of is your father when I see you."

My vision blurred. "Didn't you say I'm your best student?" I whispered.

"The most intelligent, yes. The most cunning, no. You don't listen to me when it comes to being patient and laying traps. Instead, you just barge on through. You just need to do as you're told. Al-Aasefi has gotten where he is through his ruses, not because of his intelligence. Now that he knows who you are, he can harm you. He hates you the way he hates me. He may not be able to kill me or harm me, but he can harm you. Do you know why?"

I stared at the floor.

"Because right now you still don't have any support, Nardeen. Do you know the kind of support I'm talking about? Not money, or family, or the books that you know by heart. Support here in Baghdad means power. The closer you are to Al-Rashid's palace, the safer you are."

I looked at him, turning over what Suhaib had said about Muallim Ishaq. One time he had remarked, "If he loves you—and it's a million to one chance that could happen—you'll be like his daughter. But you'll still wake up one morning to find yourself his enemy. That's what happened to me before he cut me out. He's a difficult man to understand, and that's what's always going to keep you going back to him, his mystery. He always captures the minds of the younger students, the way he speaks, his knowledge, his quirky habits. We all want to be like him."

My teacher sending me to the palace to treat Her Majesty Zubeida was worth more than money to him. What he probably wanted was for his name to be on people's tongues in the palace, which would make him more important in Bimaristan. It cut him deeply that someone like Al-Aasefi could be vice chancellor of the place. He saw himself as more deserving. At the same though, I knew he wanted to create an umbrella of protection for me by getting me close to Her Majesty Zubeida. No one could harm me if I was in her circle. Especially now since the bad blood between Al-Aasefi and my father was public, her protection was more important than ever. Muallim Ishaq finished what he was saying, "You must be somewhere safe, so that if Al-Aasefi thinks of killing you, the people of high status around you can keep an eye out for you—you'll only build relationships with such individuals by entering the palace."

We stood for a while in front of Al-Rashid's towering palace. Muallim Ishaq examined me from the top of my head to the soles of my feet. He then said, "Her Majesty is a level-headed, sensible woman. She appreciates everyone with knowledge. If you can figure out her ailment, you'll have your time in the sun. We're going to go inside now, so follow the rules of polite conversation and don't speak unless given permission."

"It's going to be impossible for me to figure out what's wrong with her."

"Nothing's impossible for my best student."

I held my breath as we walked next to the Bimaristan chancellor who had been waiting for us at the massive, vaulted doorway. Everything in Al-Rashid's palace revealed the personality of this man who worshiped all in this life that was beautiful. Book after book lined long walls, especially a lot of philosophy ones. Massive ivory-coloured pillars stretched the length of the hallways in front of us, and the floor was polished, made of the most luxurious marble. Reaching between the pillars were ornate arches shouldering the weight of the ceiling dressed in red and white, engraved with designs that you could get lost in if you looked too closely. Worlds of joy and magic in those colourful designs that almost took my breath away.

On our way to Her Majesty's majlis—her personal sitting room, everything that my eyes fell on was nothing compared to the jaw-dropping beauty of this woman. She was in her forties, from what I had heard, her face was radiant, her soft features going against what people said about her being a stiff woman. Once inside her audience chamber, the chancellor and my teacher bowed in greeting, so I did the same. Sayyid Gabriel said, "How is Your Majesty today?"

"We thank God for every day Sayyid Gabriel."

"This here is Muallim Ishaq, one of the most important doctors we have, and we've come here today with someone who can help you and help us in getting to the root of your ailment. It's Nardeen Baramika, his student, and now at your service Your Majesty."

Her Majesty Zubeida sat up straighter on the pillows in her majlis, and stared at me, her wide black eyes made even deeper by the kohl lining them. "Baramika!" she exclaimed.

An electric current shot through my body. I whipped round to Muallim Ishaq who indicated to me to keep quiet. Then he spoke to Zubeida. "Yes, from the Baramika. Her father—God rest his soul—was a brilliant doctor, and she inherited her intelligence from him. I see the same sharpness of mind and discernment in her that may help us understand your sickness and how to treat it. We have already tried seeking the advice of our nurses, but none of them could help.

This girl here, though young, has knowledge and insight that her peers don't. If you just give her a chance…"

"Who's her father?"

"My father was Hazeer the doctor," I piped up. "He and the rest of my family were murdered on Black Saturday."

I don't know how I dared speak without permission, but I knew it was my only chance to clear my father's name. My teacher wiped his sweaty palms on the sides of his robes. He tried to quiet me by interjecting, "He was one of the doctors who translated the Book of Poisons, Your Majesty."

"Ah yes, I remember it now, even the caliph himself wasn't pleased with what happened to that family. But some people are driven by rumours and anger. What a pity." She fell silent for a moment, then continued. "Very well then, very well. Let's see how skilful she is."

The Bimaristan chancellor and Muallim asked for permission to leave while I was left standing there. She asked me to come closer, so I did. Muallim had told me that she was suffering from pains in different parts of her body, making it difficult to move sometimes. He had told me to focus on specific locations on her feet. So first I examined her ankle and moved it from side to side. I asked her if doing so hurt her, and she said no. But I noticed that her big toe was swollen and when I moved it, she groaned lightly. Muallim Ishaq and Sayyid Gabriel were waiting for me outside the majlis, eager to hear what I had to say. When he saw me, Sayyid Gabriel burst out, "Back already?"

"I need to stay the whole day with her."

"An entire day? Why?"

"Some illnesses take some time for all of their symptoms to manifest," Muallim Ishaq jumped in. "Let's give her what she wants."

Sayyid Gabriel didn't seem fully convinced, but what could he do? He asked Her Majesty permission for me to accompany her for an entire day, and she agreed. While I was observing her movements, and how she groaned every time she got up or sat down, an idea came to mind—though it seemed pretty impossible. But I got the confirmation I needed when I saw the redness at every joint of her body: her ankles, her knees, her wrists. When I shared my suspicions with Sayyid Gabriel, he doubted me.

"But gout affects men more than it does women, Nardeen."

"I know, but some books say that if a woman reaches a certain age, and has the habit of eating meat every day, she could develop gout."

He paused for a moment, which made me think that he could be persuaded. So I kept going, "I'll try to reduce the pain by using ginger-soaked compresses. What do you think Sayyid Gabriel?"

"Yes, that will reduce the swelling at the points of pain. Start with that, and we'll come up with the doses of medicinal syrups. Since you started with her, I think it's best you finish this off yourself, don't leave it to the nurses."

Her Majesty didn't object at all to what I was recommending, actually she ordered her handservants to help me prepare whatever I needed and to make my coming and going from the palace as easy as possible. She really listened and made an effort to do everything I advised. One day I asked her if she ever doubted I could treat her.

"A woman is hardly inferior to a man when it comes to intellect or knowledge, Nardeen," she answered. "And an intelligent woman like me recognises a kindred spirit in you."

"Your Majesty, aren't you afraid that a Baramika is treating you?"

She broke into a wide smile, her teeth showing. She looked at me intently. "What happened between the caliph and the Baramika is part and parcel of politics. In politics there's no thought spared for blood or friendship. In politics there's one goal only, one duty, and one truth—protect and preserve the caliphate. It may seem unjust now, but people will learn, even if it is later, that the most painful decisions in politics are the most necessary ones."

Maybe she was right, maybe what happened was just part and parcel of politics that repeated itself in every time and place: victims and executioners, all pieces on a chessboard at the mercy of politics. Maybe we shouldn't judge it from the inside. Instead, we should leave the chessboard altogether and step back for a better understanding.

Muallim Ishaq was the happiest of everyone with Her Majesty Zubeida getting better. She sang his praises and insisted that he should be promoted in Bimaristan. She also gave me the most money I'd ever seen in my life. My whole time with her though, I just kept thinking of what Suhaib had said, "Don't trust Muallim!" My teacher was shocked

107

when I put all the money in his hands. He looked at me carefully and said, "This money is for you. Why are you giving it to me?"

"We don't really need this money, right?"

"So then, what do you need?"

Chapter 15

I hadn't entered the palace because my teacher had ordered me to do so, or because he had wanted to get close to Al-Rashid through me. I mean that wasn't my only goal. If Al-Aasefi was going to die in any case, that was God's will. Sure, we couldn't predict or control the timing, but we could choose how he was going to go. Would he go full of virtue and honour as he had pretended to live? Or would he be chased by shame and disgrace, making him wish that he'd died earlier? The questions that I had for Al-Aasefi, it looked like their answers would be buried with him, but I'd do my best for more than that to be buried with him. I wanted disgrace to follow his name all the way to hell.

Dirty hands are never seen, always hidden from people's eyes. You never see dirty hands, but they always leave marks that can't be wiped away. No matter how you try to remove them, they remain as evidence of the crimes that were committed. All we have to do is search for such marks and they lead us to the owners of those dirty hands. I had to go back with purpose to my plan for revenge. I was walking the tightrope between two realities. My reality was what I know Muallim to be like after all this time, and the second was Suhaib's and how he saw my teacher. At any moment I could slip off and plunge headlong into one or the other. Whatever happened there was no turning back.

I looked for Nurse Omayma everywhere in Bimaristan. When I saw her, I took her to one side and placed my hands atop hers. I squeezed them hard. Her eyes grew wide. "What's wrong Nardeen? What has happened?"

"Do you remember the slaver that bought me and then died? I want you to bring one of his servants to me."

"The slaver?! That was years ago! What made you think of him?"

I didn't have the time or patience for her questions, so I shoved some coins in her hands. She bit her lip hard when she saw how much it was, and gave it back immediately. She hung her head and stared at my feet.

"Okay, okay, I'll do it. But without all that."

The next day Nurse Omayma called me to the Bimaristan garden and there under the willow tree waiting for me was an attractive girl a few years older than me, staring indifferently at those coming and going. Omayma caught her attention then left me to it. There wasn't any time to get to know her, so I just started talking and waved a pouch of coins in front of her face. "If you answer my questions, then all of this is yours."

There was a sharp intake of breath. Her eyes grew wide and glittered at what I was offering her. "Ask me Lady, ask me!"

"Your master, the slaver who died about four years ago, tell me how he passed."

"Oh master—rest in peace—he was found in his room in the morning lying on the floor. He wasn't sick or weak or anything like that, but I guess it was his time."

"So you went inside his room?"

"Yes, me and the rest of the servants. I'll never forget what he looked like lying there."

"Was there any strange smell? I mean a sweet smell, an unusual one, something you're not used to…"

"A sweet smell…Hmm, Master used to like incense. His room was always full of different scents."

I felt my hope slipping away, and that I was right back where I started. I handed her the pouch, and she was about to leave when she blurted, "Yes, I remember now. His room was in a mess. The brass vessels on the floor and broken glass scattered everywhere. But none of us heard anything that night."

"None of you heard a thing!" I exclaimed.

Her words reminded me of what people had said about the murder of those other high-up men in Al-Rashid's court that had died under similar mysterious circumstances. They were found in a pool of blood behind closed doors, guarded by a thousand eyes. No one had heard a thing. Here I was again thrown deep into the past, memory opening its doors, creaky doors that upset hearts and made my pain swell.

Pain gives birth to hatred, which grows, puts down roots. Its features form like a foetus in the womb of pain. When such hatred comes out into the light of day, you can't say that it's ugly, because the pain that gave birth to it is uglier. People only see the pain that burns them—how selfish they can be! They don't feel the pain that rages inside each of us… they don't know that what has burned them are the flames that live in us every hour of every day. They don't know that voices, such as Suhaib's, are like fresh dew from heaven: it's what we need the most and fear the most, we, the unwelcome Baramika, left to rot in hell.

~

"I need to speak to you." Suhaib stood between me and the door leading outside of Bimaristan. I didn't have it in me to talk after everything between us having been so icy for so many days now. His arms were crossed, and he bit the inside of his cheek. And even in all that I could see he still wanted to make this work. He really did. Where did I get the strength from to push away his love? Was I really so heartless? Maybe…but I thank God that at least I had a brain, otherwise I would have hugged him in front of the whole crowd and damned them all, even with Al-Aasefi's smell on his chest and Al-Aasefi's look in his eyes, and Al-Aasefi's blood running through his veins. My brain told me off for such thoughts, so I shuffled my feet to make my way outside.

"My father wants to see you."

My stomach tightened. I found myself looking him right in the eye, "Me?"

Why would he want to see me? The last time I saw him was two days ago when the Bimaristan president announced that Muallim Ishaq would be appointed as vice president. Al-Aasefi was bubbling over with rage and accused everyone of conspiring against him. His body had been shaking and his hands waving wildly in the air. He seemed like an old lion, a lion who could barely roar anymore. Her Majesty Zubeida herself had given this order, so nothing was going to change. I had turned to my teacher and examined his face. A smile of victory was painted on his lips, delighted to see how miserable his opponent was. Almost more concerned with his win than the actual position itself, he had told Al-Aasefi, "Calm down, it's all over and done with."

"You think I'll go quietly? Hardly, no one here knows you like I do. You don't deserve such a position."

Muallim Ishaq opened his arms as far as they could go, and turned round to us, challenging Al-Aasefi. "Why don't you let everyone know what you're hiding, then? Tell them what you know about me."

Al-Aasefi had chewed his lip, like he was trying to swallow something that he would regret if he let it out. He looked to the right, then to the left, and realised just how

113

much chaos had already erupted between the doctors. Why did he throw me that look before going back to his seat? It wasn't the usual dirty look. He wanted to say something, something to do with the three of us. Maybe that's why he wanted to see me now?

Chapter 16

I walked next to Suhaib, both of us moving as slowly as possible. It was our right to steal back this time that had slipped away from us towards an unknown destiny. Just a few steps of pure love. We needed this silence that confessed everything: our wants, blaming each other, apologising. Which one of us should be apologising though? The innocent son of a murderer, or the wicked daughter of the man he killed? I had to be wicked because I dreamt of killing Al-Aasefi with my own two hands, dreamt of seeing him bleed out before me, begging, pleading for his life. That's how I imagined the end of him. My dream shrunk and shrunk even further until it disappeared before my father's angry face.

"*So you're just the same as Al-Aasefi then.*"

"*He's the reason you're dead, Baba. He took you all from me.*"

"*It's God who gives and takes away.*"

Probably God pitied me. He knew I was too weak to kill anyone, so he struck Al-Aasefi with his sickness. Sometimes we shouldn't go against fate, but instead, it's enough for us to sit back, watch and wait.

But waiting is a large stone that not every back can carry. It needs more than a strong back, it needs a heart overflowing with faith. That's what set my father apart. He was faithful, whereas my faith wobbled a lot. I had to start masking these ugly ideas of revenge and murder that thickened deep inside me and started disturbing my soul. I knew just how dark my soul had become with Suhaib's first smile. He was so good and kind that I couldn't ignore what I had become.

I snuck a look at him. I studied the corner of his mouth turning downwards. It hit me, the magnitude of the crime that we committed against Suhaib—me and Al-Aasefi—I bowed my head in sorrow and walked silently. I saw him stopping so I stopped too. "We're here," he said.

I raised my head to the home standing before me, it was more like the palace of a vizier. Guards at the door, an impressive garden. "Knowledge can't dazzle people like money does," my teacher would say. How right he was. Suhaib took two steps forward then stopped. He turned to me, his tall body blocking out everything behind him.

"Can I ask you for a favour Nardeen? It's probably the last one you'll ever do for me."

His sad tone made my heart drop. I whispered, "Anything."

"Whatever my father did to you, and whatever you've planned for him—promise me one thing. When it's all over, come back to me."

I stood, silent.

"I already lost Muallim Ishaq, and I don't want to lose you too. I'm not like Al-Aasefi, so don't be like Ishaq."

Hot tears ran down my cheeks. I didn't respond. He went on.

"I know that you're far away, caught up in the darkness of the past. I'm not asking for you to let me in there, but I'm here, asking for you to come out of it, and be here with me. Give me your hand Nardeen."

He stretched out his hand in a final attempt to persuade me, or maybe to stop me from seeing his father. He was afraid of hearing what his father had to say. Who would want to hear such truth if it was so ugly? It would probably spell the end for Suhaib and I, but I desperately needed it. I couldn't keep listening to what my heart had to say and ignoring what my mind was screaming. If I went against what my heart was saying, I'd be left with wounds to stitch up. But if I went against what my mind was telling me, I'd be full of regret. You can live with scars on your heart, but regret nibbles away at you from one hour to the next.

Do I betray my family and sell them out for love? I stretched out both of my hands and held Suhaib's palm to push it back to him. "Promises are usually broken, it's only chance that gives us more than we deserve."

Suhaib understood that I wanted to see his father whatever the cost. He went in before me, and as we walked slowly along, he led me to a room away from the rest. He knocked on the door, and we heard Al-Aasefi calling us inside. Lying down in bed, Al-Aasefi's chest rose and fell, his breathing ragged. He was dying. He tried to sit up when he saw us. Suhaib helped him do so. Al-Aasefi looked at me and I looked at him. I wanted him to know I was happy to see him so weak, even if I couldn't say it in front of Suhaib. After he stopped coughing, he spluttered, "Leave us alone, son."

"But I want to know…"

Al-Aasefi roared and his whole body shook. Afraid for him, Suhaib obeyed and closed the door behind him. His father finally turned to me fully and said, "Suhaib told me he wants you as his wife. Do you know what I told him?"

I was stunned.

"That you're no good for him. You're the daughter of a demon."

"Is that what you told people to turn them against my father? That he's a demon and so they should kill him?"

"Your father is the one who translated the Book of Poisons, so it's not too far-fetched if he would then kill someone with that knowledge. Everyone in Bimaristan thinks that."

"At least Muallim Ishaq doesn't."

"Of course, you're defending him. You're the daughter of a demon."

"My father wasn't a demon," I cried. "And we both know that my father didn't kill anyone."

"I'm not talking about your father. I'm talking about the demon that raised you."

It took me a moment to realise who he meant. My eyes felt like they would pop out. "Muallim Ishaq?"

His smirked when he caught on that I had had doubts about Muallim Ishaq. "Both of us know him well. We both know that he has more than one face. Only those who live with him and ask the right questions know who he really is."

I started sweating. Muallim Ishaq who fought for me before he even knew me. Shared his mind with me. Was my comfort and support gifted by God on that horrible night. He may have been a difficult man to understand, but he wasn't impossible to love! I had grown to love him as I did my father and had become so attached to him that he was really all I had. But the way Al-Aasefi was painting him wasn't new to me at all. I mean who can escape people's gossip? Gossip that stretches its hand around some of us, framing us however it pleases. I had never completely believed what I'd heard about him. But what I saw up close was a different matter, and it made me pause. I knew my Muallim well, but I also knew that he was a man of many faces. Al-Aasefi kept on getting into my head.

"I can't approve your union with Suhaib. How can I marry my son off to someone brought up by Ishaq? Get away from Suhaib, he's got his whole life ahead of him, and you've only got death on your hands."

"Give me the manuscript and I promise to stay away from him."

Al-Aasefi's veins were bursting against the skin on his neck. Before I knew it, his heavy hand had whipped across my face, splitting my lip, knocking me to the floor. He roared, swearing at an impossible volume. Suhaib burst in. He looked at the blood on my mouth and then at his father in disbelief.

"Father!"

"You'll never get your hands on the manuscript as long as I'm alive. Get her out of here. GET OUT NOW."

Al-Aasefi collapsed onto his bed having exhausted whatever energy he had left. Suhaib hurried to me and propped me up to take me out. When we were a bit further away from the house, I pulled my arm back and straightened up, trying to salvage whatever dignity I had left. Suhaib surprised me with what he said next.

"The manuscript that you're looking for, is it written in Syriac?"

I nodded.

Quiet for a bit, he must have been weighing up what we were about to lose. He closed his eyes. "I don't know what it says but before my father stopped me from studying with Muallim Ishaq, they had a fight about a manuscript. Muallim Ishaq asked for it, but my father refused to tell him where it was, even though I'd seen him let it go up in flames."

I gasped. "He burnt it?"

"At that time I wasn't too good at Syriac, but I made out two words: Djinn's Apple."

"Djinn's Apple? What's that?"

"It's a rare medicinal plant. How can you not know this Nardeen, when you're Ishaq's student?"

"Ishaq knows about it?"

"Of course. The manuscript definitely talked about it."

Chapter 17

Suhaib had barely finished what he was saying when I found myself sprinting to Bimaristan. I strode briskly to the library and started searching for a book that talked about this plant that for some reason Muallim never talked about during his many lectures about medicinal plants. Questions crowded my head. *Why was my father murdered for a manuscript about this medicinal plant? Why didn't Muallim tell me what the manuscript was about, and why did he deny knowing about it at all? Why would a plant like this be the reason Al-Aasefi and Ishaq are fighting?*

I didn't know how the dogs that Muallim used to take on his trips suddenly came to mind, but the next thing I knew I was reading, "And the Djinn's Apple is the mandrake. It resembles the human form and is considered sacred enough to sanctify the human spirit. If it must be uprooted from the depths of the earth, then it must be done by any hand but a human's." I breathed in a short, quick breath.

I pictured Muallim making the dogs dig out the Djinn's Apple instead of him. Reading further, it seems it was believed the plant kills anyone who uproots it. So that's why he always had to take a new dog with him on those trips, to literally do his dirty work!

The sun had nearly set, its light starting to grow faint little by little, its rays escaping through the glass windows of the library. The first cool breezes of evening swallowed up the warmth of the day. The change in light and atmosphere didn't stop me from reading further. With every page I touched, the heavy feeling in my stomach got worse. There it was: a plant with its four extensions, and a small head, all of it looking like a human, just like how it had been in Baba's manuscript on that horrific night. But instead of the questions that swirled round me that night, I was now surrounded with answers. At the bottom of the page I read: "The mandrake is mentioned in the book *The Hidden Power of Plants* more than once, for its sweet aroma, but beware because it can cause deafness." They didn't hear a thing!

So, this was the scent of death. My head hung low, I cradled it in my hands. A ferocious headache nearly split it in two. The pain felt sharper as I began to weave a new face of my teacher together with all the loose threads that were unconnected previously. I wove together all that I had heard and seen, and the words of the slave trader's servant girl came back to me, "But we didn't hear a thing."

In the pitch black of night, we owe thanks to the light of the moon. It alone washes away the heavy darkness that sits on our chests. The moon guides us and looks out for us, staying with us through the long night. I used to think that Muallim Ishaq was the moon and that I didn't want my journey to end without him, even if I was forced to ignore what everyone was saying, and how I felt deep down. Maybe he was a cold man, arrogant after all. But he had loved me like his own daughter. Was I really the daughter of a demon, then?

"You're here!"

Muallim Ishaq's voice caught me off guard. He was standing at a distance looking at me in surprise. "You didn't come home, so I grew worried. You were here the whole time?"

I closed the book and put it back in the bookcase, with a flat smile plastered across my face. "Yes, I was just reading and lost track of time."

"Let's go, it's late."

"Sure."

I said this and got closer to him. I didn't realise he saw my swollen lip. He cupped my face and tilted it upwards. "Who did this?"

My words ran away with me and I couldn't think of any lie to get out of this. I wasn't used to lying to him. Especially not when his eyes were narrowed piercing mine. My confession tumbled out. "Al-Aasefi."

"Did he come to Bimaristan today? I didn't see him."

"No, he didn't come here. I went to his house."

He looked at me sharply. "Why?"

I couldn't explain myself.

I held my head in my hand pretending to be exhausted. I knew that Muallim Ishaq wouldn't rest till he knew everything that went on between me and Al-Aasefi, but I wasn't ready to tell him. How could I, when what Al-Aasefi had said fed the doubts I already had, letting them swell more and more with every word I read about the Djinn's Apple? No, I wouldn't say anything until I figured out which of them was lying.

That night, I stayed awake. My mind was racing. Things were slowly getting clearer. But who went into the homes of such head officials in the kingdom and killed them without their guards hearing a thing? It couldn't be a demon...they can't kill anyone, they don't have the power to do so, but they can make murder possible if you already have a way. And only one person in the kingdom truly knew the ways of ancient medicine in enough depth to do this: Muallim Ishaq. *Did he kill my father too?*

Maybe because I didn't choose the beginning of the story, my hands were clean of all the blood that was spilled. But the finish to come was in my hands, and I was going to choose how it would all end.

Chapter 18

When my Muallim woke up in the morning, he found me waiting for him so that we could have breakfast together. He didn't stretch out his hand to reach for anything. Instead, he asked me, "Are you going to tell me what transpired between you and Al-Aasefi? Did he give you the manuscript?"

"No, he burnt it."

Silence fell between us. Muallim Ishaq looked at me for a while unbelievingly. He still thought it was with Al-Aasefi. He sensed the danger of me reading it. If I knew what was in it, I would turn against him—that's what he thought anyway, and so he had to get rid of it, or get rid of Al-Aasefi himself. I know my teacher well. He wouldn't wait for the hand of death, he would be the hand of death himself.

"I won't be able to make it to Bimaristan today, you go along and examine my patients."

~

When I came back that evening, he was still in his room. I called him for dinner, but he didn't answer. I was sure that he'd go out this evening, he couldn't take any more. His patience had run out and this was his chance. He wrapped himself up in his black cloak and took his basket. I prayed that he'd be in a hurry and wouldn't check what was actually in his incense burner this time. He told me not to wait for him, and I said goodbye like every other time, with a daughter's affectionate smile while he kissed the top of my head.

I had barely closed my eyes when pounding on the door made me sit up suddenly in bed. The person knocking didn't give me a chance to collect myself, and just kept pounding. I ran barefoot to the door, opened it a crack, and Sayyida Aidiya fell in wailing and screaming.

"The guards have arrested Muallim Ishaq at someone's house. O God! People are saying he was carrying a poisoned dagger. Was he planning on murdering the man?"

She hugged me and started to comfort me teary-eyed. Our prayers overlapped, each of us hoping for his safety, but each of us for our own reasons. She wanted her neighbour safe and sound, and I wanted my father's killer alive. I wanted to close the final door in the room of my memories of that night: why did he kill my father?'

The news spread in Bimaristan like wildfire. Al-Aasefi was found in a pool of his own blood, and at his head was Muallim Ishaq. Why? How? No one could be certain. On that night, those in the household had woken up to a scream from Al-Aasefi, and when they ran to him room, they found Muallim Ishaq there. There, with a dagger in his hand, and a surprised look on his face. He didn't expect anyone to hear Al-Aasefi's scream. He thought none of them would hear a thing even if Al-Aasefi had screamed enough to make the sky fall. But they heard him. He had tried to inspect the incense burner but the guards led him outside of the house. He probably wanted to see me, just as I wanted to see him.

"Don't go to him," Suhaib spat.

"I've got to go. I'll always be stuck in the past if I don't see him."

No one was allowed to see him, but Muallim had told me once that, "In Baghdad your network is your power." I asked Her Majesty Zubeida to help me organise a visit. I was finally able to visit him in prison.

The prison was on the outskirts of the city, and I was lost in my thoughts as the carriage travelled along deserted streets. In the twilight the thick stone prison walls stretched far into the sky with only a handful of tiny windows. The guards were expecting me, and as I alighted, immediately lead me into the prison. It was a dreadful place, the stench almost unbearable, the screams and banging on walls and doors pounding my head. But then we walked through a stone archway, across a courtyard and into another wing. Here there were no screams or smells, and only one prisoner sat in the shadows of the lantern placed outside his cell. I was carrying some of his clothes, books and his golden ring with the blue gemstone. He had left it behind on the table and it would be wrong for him to be without it.

"You may leave us," I said to the guard who hesitated for a minute but left in a hurried manner as I pointed at the door.

Muallim was in one of the corners curled up on the stone floor. I approached him, the cell dim—the only light coming through a small window near the ceiling. He raised his eyes to look at me. They narrowed trying to figure out who was standing in front of him. I heard the cell door close behind me. I checked to see that the guard was still close by. Placing Muallim's belongings in front of him on the ground, I said, "Baba suspected that you were using the Djinn's Apple to kill people. Right?"

He stretched his hand out to the golden ring and considered it. "He didn't just know, he was going to give the manuscript to the caliph himself and ruin everything. Al-Aasefi and I would have been killed. We were just trying to save our own skins, nothing else." He slipped the ring on his little finger with some difficulty. "What did you put in the incense burner Nardeen? It wasn't Djinn's Apple paste, so what was it?"

"Some other herbs that smell just like Djinn's Apple, but don't have the same effect."

Muallim Ishaq smiled and leaned his head against the wall. "It's not surprising that the guards caught me before I could clean up...but I'm proud of you Nardeen. At least I've made sure that you're like me."

"Not at all! I've never killed anyone. I'm not like you at all Ishaq. You killed Al-Aasefi, my father, and more. As for me, when I marry Suhaib and we start a family, I'll make sure that no one ever links us to you ever again."

"But you are a killer, Nardeen." He said this and pulled the gemstone out of his ring, put it in his mouth, and started chewing. "If you take the paste of the Djinn's Apple and drain it of its juice, you'll be left with a small ball the size of a gemstone, with enough poison in it to kill five men. Wrap it up and keep it with you always. Do you see now? You brought death here to me."

I felt my eyes straining out of their sockets and my heartbeat pounding, while Ishaq kept chewing on the poison that I had unknowingly just handed him. Before closing his eyes, he smiled. "You chose to be like me. And I chose to be a demon. Maybe you regret it all now, but I don't regret any of it."

Epilogue

I'm sitting at the large window in Baba's study as the afternoon light fades, I stroke my swollen belly. The scent of blossoms and herbs is in the air. I can see Shuaib and little Samira running around together in the garden. Their infectious laughter floats up to me, and my heart aches to run down to them. They are my deepest loves.

Everything is back in its place on the shelves. The books, the large table in the middle, Baba's pens, his mortar and pestle, his incense burner. I keep thinking Baba will walk through the door any time now and start discussing his patients with me. I'd have so much to say to him. And little Bayan, who would be all grown up. And Mama, what would you say, would you be proud of me? Or angry that a Baramika girl is treating so many people, especially the poor, as Baba used to do? Would Rohan and Laween be renowned doctors with their own families?

It's been three years since Muallim's death, and our last moment together is etched deep in my memories. In all the things that passed to me from him—his cherished books, his notes, his medical instruments—were four rings. I recall their shimmer, how the blue stones glinted under the golden light of the lamp. Four rings, crafted with the Djinn's Apple. They are mine now. I have put them away, in a secret place even Shuaib does not know about. I will keep them with me always. I'll use them to protect my family, whatever the cost.

Glossary

Abbasids—Rulers during the Abbasid period, 750 to 1258 CE

Agie—police headquarters

Al-Rashid / Harun Al-Rashid—The ruler of Baghdad at this time

Allahu Akbar—God is great

Baramika—Renowned noble family

Bayt-Al-Hikma—House of Knowledge

Bimaristan—Hospital

Binti—Endearing term for daughter

Caliph—Ruler

Child of Yahya Al-Baramika—Yahya Al-Baramika was a high ranking official in the Abbasid courts

Dodonaea—A genus of flowering plants

Ebers papyrus—Egyptian medical papyrus of herbal knowledge dating to c. 1550 BCE

Five prayers—Daily Islamic prayers

La hawla wa la quwata illa billah—There is no power and no
strength except with God

Majlis—Official sitting room where formal meetings are
held

Muallim—Teacher

Musa bin Ja'far—Harun Al-Rashid's cousin

Surah—A chapter in the Quran. There are 114 surahs in the
Quran

Thawb—Usually white ankle-length robe, with long sleeves
worn by men

Harun Al-Rashid: The Golden Age of Baghdad

Harun Al-Rashid is one of the most famous caliphs in Islamic history. He ruled the Abbasid caliphate from 786 to 809 CE, and his reign is often considered to be the golden age of Baghdad. He is also known for his association with the famous stories of the 1001 Nights. While the stories themselves are fictional, they are set in the Abbasid period and are said to be based on the exploits of Harun Al-Rashid and his court. During his time, Baghdad was a center of trade, learning, and the arts.

Baghdad was home to a diverse population of Muslims, Jews, and Christians, and other religious groups, and it was a crossroads for ideas from all over the world. The Abbasid caliphs were patrons of the arts and sciences, and they founded many libraries and institutions of higher learning. The House of Wisdom in Baghdad was one of the most famous libraries in the world, and it housed a vast collection of books and manuscripts on a wide range of subjects. Scholars from all over the Islamic world came to Baghdad to study and research, and the city became a major center of intellectual activity.

Harun Al-Rashid was himself a cultured man, and he was interested in all aspects of learning. He was a patron of poets, musicians, and artists, and he was also a keen collector of books and manuscripts. He was known for his lavish lifestyle, and his court was a center of opulence and luxury.

Despite the cultural and intellectual achievements of Harun Al-Rashid's reign, it was also a time of political intrigue. The caliph was often challenged by his own family members, by powerful military leaders and by other neighbouring dynasties, like the Ummayads. In 796, he was forced to move his capital from Baghdad to Raqqa, in Syria, in order to escape the political turmoil in the city.

Harun Al-Rashid's reign also saw the rise of the Baramikas, a powerful family of Persian viziers. The Baramikas were instrumental in helping Harun Al-Rashid to consolidate his power, but they eventually fell out of favor with the caliph. In 803, Harun Al-Rashid had the Baramikas executed, and their deaths plunged the empire into a period of political instability.

The Bimaristan

"Bimaristan" refers to hospitals in the medieval Islamic world, with the term derived from the Persian word for "place of the sick".

The bimaristan in Baghdad during Harun Al-Rashid's was one of the most advanced hospitals in the world. It was founded in the late 8th century by the caliph's vizier, Jibrail ibn Bukhtyishu. The hospital was staffed by a team of doctors, surgeons, and pharmacists, and it offered a wide range of medical services.

The bimaristan was likely an imposing structure built with local materials such as baked brick and limestone. It would have been well-appointed, given the importance of the institution. The complex would likely have included a central courtyard, reflecting the typical architectural style of the Islamic world. The entrance may have been adorned with intricate geometric and arabesque patterns, typical of Islamic architecture.

Inside, the bimaristan was designed to maximize natural light and airflow, making it a comfortable environment for patients. Rooms were typically arranged around the central courtyard. Separate wards existed for different diseases, and there were rooms for surgical procedures, pharmacies, and accommodations for staff and visiting family.

The bimaristan may have also included a library, given the Abbasid Caliphate's emphasis on learning and scholarship. The interiors would have been decorated with tile work, calligraphy, and plaster reliefs. A water source or fountain was likely present in the central courtyard for ablution and cooling the environment.

The bimaristan was also known for its high standards of hygiene. The Abbasids understood the connection between cleanliness and health, so the bimaristan would have had well-maintained facilities for waste disposal and regular cleaning.

The emphasis was on creating a space that not only healed the body but also the mind and soul. Therefore, the bimaristan was typically surrounded by gardens and greenery, providing a tranquil environment for recovery.

The bimaristan had specialist wards for general medicine, surgery, ophthalmology, and pediatrics. The hospital also had a library, a pharmacy, and a research center. It was a place of great learning and innovation. Doctors at the hospital developed new treatments for diseases, and they also made important contributions to the field of surgery. The bimaristan was also a center of medical education, and it attracted students from all over the Islamic world.

The hospital was a symbol of the caliph's commitment to public health and welfare. It was a place where people could receive quality medical care, regardless of their social status. It was also a center of medical research and innovation, and it helped to make Baghdad a leading center of learning in the Islamic world.

The bimaristan in Baghdad was a significant achievement in the history of medicine. It was one of the first hospitals in the world to offer a comprehensive range of medical services. The bimaristan helped to make Baghdad a leading center of learning in the Islamic world, and it had a lasting impact on the development of medicine.

About the Author

Djamila Morani is an Algerian novelist and an Arabic language professor. Her first novel, released in 2015 and titled *Taj el-Khatiaa*, is set in the Abbasid period (like *The Djinn's Apple*), but in Kazakhstan. All of her works thus far are deeply rooted in untold histories. *The Djinn's Apple* is her first full-length work published in English.

About the Translator

Sawad Hussain is a translator from Arabic whose work has been recognised by English PEN, the Anglo-Omani Society and the Saif Ghobash Banipal Prize for Arabic Literary Translation, among others. She is a judge for the Palestine Book Awards and the 2023 National Translation Award. She has run translation workshops under the auspices of Shadow Heroes, Africa Writes, Shubbak Festival, the Yiddish Book Center, the British Library and the National Centre for Writing. Her most recent translations include *Black Foam* by Haji Jaber (AmazonCrossing) and *What Have You Left Behind* by Bushra al-Maqtari (Fitzcarraldo Editions). She was selected to be the Princeton Translator in Residence in 2025. Her website is: www.sawadhussain.com

Reader's Guide

1. Loss and grief are key themes in *The Djinn's Apple*. How did the loss of Nardeen's family shape her character and influence her quest for justice?

2. Did you connect with Nardeen's character? Was she someone you rooted for throughout the entire novel, or were there times when you disagreed with her?

3. The author intertwines themes of crime, history, and magic. Which theme resonated with you the most, and why?

4. How did the magical elements contribute to the overall atmosphere of the story? Did they add a layer of intrigue or alter your expectations of how the mystery would unfold?

5. What did you learn about the Abbasid period? Which elements of Abbasid society surprised or intrigued you the most?

6. How did your impression of Shuaib change as the story unfolded? What do you believe the romance between Nardeen and Shuaib adds to the overall narrative?

7. How do you feel about the book's resolution, particularly regarding the fate of Muallim Ishaq? Do you believe there was justice for the murder of Nardeen's family?

8. What is your understanding of the political backdrop of the setting? Is there anything you found particularly interesting that you would like to learn more about?

9. What is your interpretation of the epilogue? What do you think the future holds for Nardeen?

10. Reflect on the illustrations at the start of each chapter. Did you notice any clues as you were reading the story? Discuss how each clue is relevant to the murder mystery.

About English PEN

English PEN is one of the world's oldest human rights organisations, championing the freedom to write and the freedom to read around the world. It is the founding centre of PEN International, a worldwide writers' association with 130 centres in more than 90 countries.

With the support of its members—a community of writers, readers and activists—English PEN protects freedom of expression whenever it is under attack. It campaigns for writers facing persecution around the world and offers respite residencies for 3-5 writers per year.

English PEN celebrates contemporary international writing through its online magazine, *PEN Transmissions*, and awards literary grants for translating new works into English.

It brings together outstanding writers, readers and translators for unforgettable conversations and celebrates courageous writing with two annual literary prizes—the PEN Pinter Prize and the PEN Hessell-Tiltman Prize.

Supported using public funding by

ARTS COUNCIL ENGLAND

About the Award

PEN Translates was launched in 2012, with support from Arts Council England, to encourage UK publishers to acquire more books from other languages. The award helps UK publishers to meet the costs of translating new works into English—whilst ensuring translators are acknowledged and paid properly for their work.